World Football Domination

The Virtual Talent Scout

Volume 1

Anthony Ranieri

i

Dedication

This book is dedicated to the great Australian football legend Johnny Warren. His love and admiration for all people and cultures that participate in the world game will last forever.

ANTHONY RANIERI

Contents

ANTHONY RANIERI

Acknowledgments

Writing a novel about the sport I love is one of the most significant projects I have ever committed to completing. It was different from the genre I had written about before (which was job hunting) and represented many challenges. I want to acknowledge my wife, Erma, for her patience and tolerance for the many hours I spent in coffee shops writing my first draft. I also want to thank my children for inspiring me to write about a sport that has always brought us together.

I want to thank my book cover designer, Momir Borocki, for designing a stunning visual for the front cover. I want to offer my gratitude to Sally Bird from Calidris Literary Agency for her feedback during my draft preparation. She has always been a great mentor, and I was fortunate enough to leverage her writing expertise.

I want to acknowledge Australian Writers' Centre for critiquing parts of the book. I learned so much from their experience and knowledge.

Although I am the author of this book, I am not a singular entity. I recognise that it was the kindness of the people around that motivated me to complete it.

Foreword

It's a great honour to be asked to write the foreword to Anthony Ranieri's science fiction football book, *World Football Domination—The Virtual Talent Scout: Volume 1*. Anthony is a devoted, knowledgeable, and passionate football man who cares deeply about doing what is in the best interest of the game. In my opinion, these attributes would most certainly classify him as what Johnny Warren would have called a "true believer."

I first met Anthony after my uncle and godfather, Australian football legend Johnny Warren, sadly passed away in 2004. During our meeting, Anthony said he was a great admirer of Johnny's and that as a child of Italian immigrants, he loved the way John had stood up for the game and people who felt discriminated against, simply because they loved and played the most popular game on the planet, football. Anthony said Johnny had had an immense influence on him and was an inspiration while he was growing up playing football.

World Football Domination is a title that goes hand in hand with Johnny's dream of an Australian team winning the FIFA World Cup. The book's aspirational tones remind me of Johnny and his inspiring statements, such as, "It's time we stopped talking about qualifying for the World Cup and started talking about winning it," and "If Greece can win the European Championships and Turkey and South Korea can make the semi-finals of the 2002 World Cup, then there's a message there for Australia. Champion teams can beat a team of champions. Call me a dreamer." Of course, Australia has since gone on to become AFC Asian Cup champions in both the women's (China 2010) and men's (Australia 2015) divisions, while the Western Sydney Wanderers won the Asian Champions League in 2014. The World Cup victories await!

World Football Domination is a thoroughly enjoyable book that highlights the success of a small nation like Iceland (population: 334,000) (Wikipedia, 2019) on the world stage in recent years. They have been ranked number twenty-one in the men's FIFA/Coca-Cola World Ranking and number nineteen in the women's FIFA World Rankings, while the men's team qualified for the 2016 European Championship and the first World Cup in Russia.

Is it something in the water, or do they have top-secret, innovative, state-of-the-art technology leading them to world football success? And can Australian football get in on the act?

My life has unsurprisingly revolved around football from as young as I can remember. My father, Ross Warren, the eldest of the Warren brothers, played with Johnny and their other brother, Geoff, at St George Budapest Soccer Club. When he retired from playing after breaking his leg, he went on to a successful coaching career with the St George second- and third-grade sides, Arncliffe Scots and Wollongong Wolves youth teams. I can remember as a young child going to many of the Budapest training sessions at Carss Park, Kogarah, and many New South Wales first-division games at Hurstville Oval and the Sydney Sports Ground (now Allianz Stadium).

I started playing as a four-year-old in the under 8s with the Peakhurst/Lugarno Soccer Club and progressed to playing representative football in the Illawarra region of NSW after my parents relocated from Sydney to Kiama on the south coast of NSW. After the Wollongong Wolves were founded, I continued to play in their junior representative teams as well as being selected in the NSW state teams for under 13s to under 18s.

In 1984, Uncle Johnny took me to Brazil on a six-week football study tour, which included a trial at Clube de Regatas do Flamengo (a.k.a. Flamengo). It was the most supported club in Brazil, with 45 million supporters, and it was the club of Brazilian football god Zico. The multiple

FIFA World Cup championship winner Mario Zagallo was the first-team coach, and the Maracanã Stadium was their home ground.

After the trial, Flamengo asked me to sign for them, as they thought I had the potential to become a professional footballer. I stayed in Rio de Janeiro for six months, training every day and playing with the Flamengo under 16 team before returning to Australia. I continued my career with the Wollongong Wolves and then the St George club. In 1986, I was awarded a Big Brother Movement Scholarship and trained at Manchester United for one month with the likes of England captain Bryan Robson and Scottish international player Gordon Strachan under the coaching of Sir Alex Ferguson. The late Eric Harrison, the renowned Manchester United youth team coach, was the coach of the apprentice team and in charge of youth development at that time.

Unfortunately, a series of broken legs curtailed my playing ambitions and forced me to think of pursuing an education and a career other than playing professionally. So I enrolled in a bachelor of business in tourism program and completed the course in 2004 after seven years. I was running our family business, the Jamberoo Pub, as well as studying and raising a young family with my wife, Cheryl. We have two children, Jordan, who is twenty-one years of age, and Gemma, who is seventeen. I am still studying and currently enrolled in a master of business administration program, as I now value the opportunities a quality education and lifelong learning creates.

As the children were growing up, I started coaching them at the Kiama Junior Football Club. I completed all the required junior community coaching courses as well as the FFA Advanced C and B Licences. It was a very steep learning curve for me, as I had always viewed the game from a playing perspective. Now I had the important position of being a role model and influencer of sixteen kids and their parents. The goal at the community level was to teach the kids the basics and make sure they spent every possible second with the ball, and I had to do my best to ensure they enjoyed the sport. I signed up the following year. As I started to improve my coaching skills, I was lucky enough to coach at the elite youth level with the Wollongong Wolves.

Johnny Warren saw youth development and coaching education as necessary for Australian football if the league wanted to achieve at the highest level. *World Football Domination* raises many issues that Johnny used to advocate for, namely the need for a world-class technical director who could implement a peerless coach education system and pathways to that career. He also saw the necessity for quality scouting and talent identification, lower player fees, and increased use of futsal for player development, and recommended a significant focus on scouting and development of indigenous players.

The 6th of November 2019 will be the fifteenth anniversary of Johnny Warren's passing. So many improvements have been made to football since his death. However, the advances in technology since 2004 have been immense. In the early 2000s, Johnny had only just started to use a laptop with internet and email. Back then, if someone had mentioned using a drone to remotely scout players and send that information back to a desktop computer thousands of kilometres away to be analysed, we would have thought they were mad.

Imagine players from indigenous communities that could be scouted and developed into professional players, Matildas and Socceroos, with the top-secret Icelandic drone technology! How many players from those communities don't play the game or choose to play Rugby League or Australian Rules Football instead? And many of them don't participate in any sport at all. So how much football talent is lost from those communities? How many of those children have the potential to represent their communities at clubs around the world, such as Barcelona, Flamengo, Liverpool, Boca Juniors, Real Madrid,

Manchester United, Bayern Munich, AC Milan, and Juventus? Perhaps one of the many ambitious and successful Asian clubs from Japan, China, or South Korea? Imagine using the technology to scout and develop indigenous players to the level of being good enough to win the World Cup, the European Champions League, or the Copa Libertadores de América

Potentially, Australia has a future Ballon d'Or winner in these communities; it's the oldest living culture in the world with 60,000 years of stories to tell. Imagine what world football domination could do for indigenous communities and generational change, as well as for the broader Australian community.

I would like to sincerely thank Anthony Ranieri for the opportunity to contribute to *World Football Domination—The Virtual Talent Scout: Volume 1*. I love his passion for the game and his ability to dream, and I wish him every success on his never-ending football journey.

—Jamie Warren, executive chairman
Johnny Warren Football Foundation

1 | The Scouting Revolution

When I'm up in the big football field in the sky, I just want people to remember, I told you so.

Johnny Warren, soccer legend

Circa 2050

A crimson sky with touches of blue and green haze hung in the distance as the sunset slowly descended over the chilly Icelandic capital. It was a light show unlike anything seen outside this northernmost capital of the world. The lights swished and swirled with uniform motion as though choreographed to perfection. They changed intensity with a touch of softness reminiscent of a throwaway silk blanket. Although it was a typically cold day in Reykjavík and heading into the fearless winter season, the light show provided a sense of warmth and security. Was it a trick to make you think that winter in Iceland wasn't as bad as people thought?

Robby Denehy watched the sunset through his taxi window. He loved the fierce beauty of the country. He was visiting the city of Reykjavík for the launch of a revolutionary football scouting technology that would change world football talent identification forever. He was eagerly awaiting this seminar with a flurry of other football technical experts from around the world. He was on his way to the Icelandair Reykjavík Hotel Natura, where enthusiastic patrons from all over the globe would be staying.

He was travelling by taxi from Keflavík International Airport to Reykjavík. The unattractive barren landscape alongside the road was unassuming and synonymous with this drive. The arctic chill met with every breath that he exhaled from his mouth. It was like opening the freezer, and a blast of cold air penetrated your face each time without forgiveness. However, he didn't have the option to close the door and be done with it.

As the taxi reached the outskirts of Reykjavík, he noticed something unusual that prompted his interest. He asked the taxi driver to slow down to get a better view of it.

"Stop here, please!"

It was a well-developed football training facility, with multiple playing fields and a large building for indoor playing. An extensive pipe network emanating from underground stood out like an industrial statue. He had read about the expansive natural underground steam system that powered the Icelandic energy grid. He opened his window and heard an unusual buzzing sound above.

I am too far from the airport for planes to be flying around, he thought.

He looked into the sky. To his puzzlement, there was a large drone flying above the playing field. It manoeuvred its way into the middle of the pitch and then remained stationary, undisturbed by the Icelandic gusts of wind.

What on earth is going on here? he thought.

Below the drone, two people in beanies and heavily padded black jackets stood next to an on-field control hub. One person was controlling the drone with a joystick, and the other was monitoring it from a computer. To his curiosity, this was all going on while a group of at least twenty players participated in a high-tempo match on a restricted-size playing field. It was a well-structured football trial. He looked closer and noticed all the players wearing a fitted armband on their right shoulders.

He quickly opened the taxi door, wanting to get a closer look. "I'm going to step outside for a few minutes," he said to the driver while pointing towards the playing field.

He walked briskly, firmly clutching his jacket. Not far in front of him, flickering red, yellow, and green lights were pulsating from the drone. Simultaneously, green lights intermittingly pulsated on the players' armbands at high speeds. It resembled a light circus, and the night had transformed into a high-tech visual display. Red, green, blue, and white, flicker, flicker, flicker; it was unbelievable. He felt hypnotised but was still able to control his senses.

The well-lit playing field had modern light towers and high fencing surrounding it. As he approached the fence perimeter, one of the technicians manoeuvred the drone towards him. He waved his hands in the air to get his attention and then dropped them, realising it was pointless.

The drone was getting louder, and the purring sound had changed into a high-pitched electric screech. It was changing direction and moving towards him, slowly at first as it swung around. He started to sense this wasn't going to be a friendly encounter and began to feel concerned. He instinctively put his right arm over his eyes to protect himself from the glaring lights of the drone.

He stood motionless as the drone's powerful lights securely focused on his face, forcing him to duck his head to avoid the intense glare. As the drone manoeuvred away from him and paled insignificance, it released a burst of smelly white smoke. It had the stench of mustard and dirty, rotten apples that were close to fermentation. The drone was designed to protect itself if someone wanted to tamper with it. It didn't affect his eyes or skin, but he had to cover his mouth with his jacket. Robby resembled a bandito on the run. He placed his hands over his ears to relieve the excruciating sound that was still coming from the drone.

Had he stumbled onto something he wasn't supposed to? The piercing sound and bright lights were all too much for him as he turned around and walked briskly towards the taxi waiting fifty metres away. Huffing and puffing, he took deep breaths as he finally made it to the vehicle. He looked up to be greeted by a tall man standing next to the passenger door. He had a grey beard and was wearing a black beanie similar to the technicians controlling the drone.

"Can I ask what you are doing here?" he asked in a strange English accent.

"I'm sorry to cause any problems, but I wanted to see the drone. I'm a football scout here for the conference, and I was curious."

"OK. I'm sorry to startle you, sir, but this is a closed session, and visitors are not allowed without permission."

"Yeah, no worries." Robby was unnerved by the experience.

"There have been people spying on our new technology, so we get nervous when someone pulls up in a car and walks towards the football field."

"I understand. Sorry again."

"I need to check your identity papers. Do you have a passport?"

"Are you the police? Why do you need to see my passport?"

"I am not the police, sir. We are security guards for this facility." He directly looked at Robby with piercing eyes. "I can call the police, if you prefer, for further questioning, or you can provide me with your passport, and I can let you on your way."

He was unsure what to do next. He didn't want to end up in a police station the day before the conference.

"Fine. It's in my document wallet . . . one moment." He fidgeted, searching his pockets until he finally found the wallet. "Here you are . . . my passport."

The security guard flashed his torchlight on the document and then suspiciously looked at him several times. "I think we are going to be OK this time, Mr Denehy.' He handed the passport back to him. "Enjoy your stay in Iceland." He placed his hand on his shoulder. "By the way, I don't want this to happen again. I hope you understand."

"I get it, don't worry. I think I will be on my way now."

The security guard nodded and turned away into the night.

It was getting late, and the taxi driver also was keen to move on. Robby's curiosity had gotten the best of him but for the right reasons. He was a well-credentialed football talent scout, and what he had witnessed had stirred his senses. He had never seen anything like it before. Something was going on in this small country that might explain its rapid rise in world football rankings. He wanted to know more, but it would have to wait until the next day.

By the time he made it to his hotel room, he was done. He had been awake for twenty-five hours, and he barely noticed the tasteful nautical-chic décor. He wanted two things: a beer and to lie down on something that didn't move or squash his six-foot frame.

He pulled a beer from the fridge and stared out the window at Mount Esja in the distance. A mouthful convinced him that he needed to move to Iceland. He read the label: "Viking. Something boutique and local." It tasted like the gods had dropped it off on their way to Valhalla. It was different than the beers back home. Not so processed, with a pure and refreshing taste.

He relaxed his slender frame by sprawling over the neo-modern couch, his long, skinny legs stretched out and his feet resting on the retro stool. He was in his comfort zone. The blue Adidas jacket with the Australian football logo was zipped up to his neck. He was a branded man and loved his Adidas gear. With his arms folded across his chest, he considered what the next day would bring. It had been a long trip from his Australian homeland on the other side of the world. He was a tired man that needed a solid rest.

He placed his mobile phone on the side table, and new message prompts greeted him. He finally had gotten reception, and all his communications from the past twenty-four hours were coming in at once. He scrolled through the first five messages and then gave up. There were contracts for agents to sign and requests to scout players. He was already two weeks behind in his work, and it was overwhelming. All he wanted was a good night's sleep for now. The messages could wait.

As the sun descended into the horizon, the crimson sky gave way to the power of the night. With his eyes half-open, the Viking beer started to take effect as he dozed off in the comfort of his Nordic-style couch.

The next day, breakfast was being served in the main dining room, and it was overflowing with patrons from around the world. The hotel was abuzz and struggling to keep up with the demands of its guests. Some were becoming agitated and restless, for it was taking a while for their food to arrive. Robby had an easy-going nature that was typical of his Australian upbringing, and it did not bother him. He managed to find an empty seat in an awkward spot near the back of the dining room. Because it was adjacent to the noisy kitchen, nobody wanted it.

He looked scruffy: hair uncombed, unshaven, with his clothes showing creases all over. He wore the same Adidas jacket, which looked like it had been tossed around on the floor and stomped on several times. As he sipped on his lukewarm skinny latte, he noticed a familiar face not far from his table. He looked again to make sure and squinted his bright-blue eyes several times. It was Liam McHenry from the Scottish Football Federation. Their friendship went back a long way, and they first had met twenty years ago when they had played football together in the Scottish Premier League. They both had become football scouts and established experts in their field. The last time they had met was two years ago during a training conference in Switzerland.

They caught each other's eye, and with a cheeky smile, he waved to his old friend.

"Hi, Liam. Why don't you come and sit here?" he shouted across the room.

Liam waved his hands in acknowledgment and made his way towards him. He ducked around the tables and chairs of the overcrowded room and eventually took a seat. They firmly shook hands and greeted each other with enthusiasm, patting each other on the back.

Liam was a towering man at 1.9 metres tall, and it had served him well as a centre forward during his prime as a professional football player. He had scored many goals for his club due to his height and ability to leap above defenders with regularity. It had made him a menace to opposing teams.

He was the leading goal scorer in his first season with twenty-five goals, followed by a spectacular second season with twenty-eight goals. Liam was a freak centre forward, a player that only popped up once every decade. He had had the world in the palm of his hands and continuously received offers from big clubs around Europe. However, his career had ended prematurely due to a crunching tackle that broke his leg in two places. As so happens with many talented footballers, this lofty, blond-haired Scotsman who was the darling of many supporters had his career ended on short notice. A career destroyed in one moment by an opposing player executing a deliberate tackle intended to inflict pain and suffering.

"How are you, my good old Australian mate? It's been a long time." He patted Robby on the back again. "I never expected to see you here."

"It's great to see you again . . . and you have gone places since we last met." Robby could not curtail his excitement. "I heard about your promotion.

Congratulations!"

"It's a big job, mate. My family complains I am never home." Liam adjusted his seat, facing away from the kitchen, and placed his hands on the table. "I'm looking forward to going home after this conference and on an overdue vacation."

"I understand entirely, and look at me—I'm from the arse end of the world. I guess you're here to see the player identification system like everyone else?"

"Oh, yes. I'm excited about what I have read so far." Liam paused. "I managed to get trial data from my contacts, and it looks encouraging. But I am interested in your thoughts." He folded his arms.

"Iceland is a small country with a population of just over 350,000, and their achievements have been phenomenal." Robby took a deep breath and then sipped on his coffee. "How else could you explain their consistent ranking in the top ten nations in the world? They have a long list of players applying their trade in the top tiers of European competition."

"I couldn't agree with you more, my good friend. There have been some good results from the trial data." He was definitely in the know. "They already have identified two local Icelandic players of exceptional talent that have apprenticeships in the English Premier League, and there is more in the pipeline in their local competition."

"I also have seen the data, and I must admit, it's impressive." Robby was expecting big things from this revolution in talent identification. "We could be on a hell of a ride if what I think is possible."

"How did you get the data, mate?" Liam was curious.

"You know me. I wasn't going to travel this far without some evidence, so I was provided with a confidential snapshot by the conference organiser."

Liam smiled. "If anyone could get that information, it would be you!"

"I had to sign a confidentiality agreement. So if I tell you anything, I must kill you!"

"Ha, ha. I don't want you to kill me, so no need to tell me anything."

"I must confess, though. I witnessed something coming from the airport. It was extraordinary," Robby said.

He had Liam's full attention, as he liked getting the inside scoop. "What is it, mate? I can see that curiosity in your eyes, so tell me."

Robby leaned forwards and lowered his tone to almost a whisper. "I was on my way to the hotel from the airport and passing by a football training facility visible from the main road."

"Tell me, what did you see?"

"You're going to think I'm nuts, but I stumbled onto a drone flying above the football pitch while players were performing an intense training session."

"What?" Liam's eyebrows stretched upwards.

"Yeah, two guys were controlling the whole thing below and monitoring its performance from a computer hub."

"You're kidding me."

"I don't think I was meant to be there and was asked to leave by a security guy."

"Geez, that's an experience!" Liam wanted to know more.

"I have never seen anything like it before . . . the technology, I mean," Robby said.

"I know curiosity always got the best of you."

"Something is going on in Iceland with their system of football development." Robby waited to get his breath back. "I can assure you it's unlike anything I have experienced before."

"That's a big call from you."

"I'm hoping the conference today may shed some light on it. But in the meantime, how about you and I keep this story to ourselves?"

Liam smiled with a two-finger salute. "You can trust me. Scout's honour."

The conference was about to start in twenty minutes.

The foyer of the hotel was abuzz with patrons eagerly waiting for the presentation by Gunnar Grimsson. He was a world expert in sports engineering and had developed a reputation for innovative and progressive thinking in player talent identification. He was attached to the Icelandic Football Federation as an individual consultant on player development, and his record for identifying great athletes was remarkable.

"The conference organiser is calling everyone in from the foyer," Robby said. "We better start making our way."

They followed the line of people leaving the dining area to the foyer outside the main entrance. Before entering the auditorium, three tall security guards in black uniforms and military-style caps stood at both doors checking passes before letting anyone in. It was unusual to have a security presence at these forums, and usually, people were free to move around. These guys were serious; they were thorough as they checked bags for cameras and recording devices.

Robby waited his turn, only to realise that the security guard in front of him was the same person that had confronted him at the football field yesterday.

That looks like him, he thought.

As Robby cleared security, they both looked at each other with a half-smile. They did not want to make it obvious they had had a previous encounter.

Robby took his seat near the large windows facing the bay. It was a great view of Reykjavík Harbour, and he immersed himself in the picturesque setting. The sun's rays spectacularly filtered through the auditorium's tall windows, creating a sense of warmth and anticipation. It was nature's way of putting on a show, a prelude to a special event.

As the patrons took their seats, the organiser called for their attention. A welcoming message scrolled across the main screen at the front of the auditorium in Icelandic: *Velkomin to Islana*— "Welcome to Iceland."

"Ladies and gentlemen of the football fraternity, I welcome you all to this special event in Reykjavík. In Iceland, you are all considered part of our football family, and I welcome you with open arms. It's the first time the Icelandic Football Federation has sponsored such an event in our country, and your presence today has been enthusiastic. It's a full house!

"Gunnar Grimsson, the inventor of our virtual talent identification technology, will present a remarkable achievement in football talent identification. Known as PVI—Player Virtual Identification—this system has been operational in Iceland for two years and has produced remarkable results. Without further ado, I present to you Gunnar Grimsson."

All the patrons stood up enthusiastically with a round of applause, smiling as Gunnar made his way to the podium. He was a monster of a man, standing nearly two meters tall, lean and lanky.

"Ladies and gentlemen of the football fraternity, I welcome you all to Iceland, and as you can see, it's not an inhospitable place, as some people would like you to believe," Gunnar said. "The sun is shining, and there is not a cloud in sight. But let me warn you, it won't last very long. Wait until this afternoon when the clouds roll in."

The audience chuckled. Gunnar was known to have a charismatic personality.

"Let me challenge you all today as football experts with experience in identifying talent. How many of you can honestly say that the talent you have identified in the past has been the best and the only football players available for you to consider? What I mean is, how often has potential talent gone unidentified? It's a question I want you to think about in the context of the PVI system. I also know it's a question that haunts a number of you in your profession."

Gunnar paused and sipped on a glass of water as he waited for the patrons to think about his questions.

"To identify talented players, many things have to happen all at once, and it's like all the planets aligning at the same time. You have to be at the right place at the right time when the player is outperforming right in front of you. But what if that player wasn't there because their parents were too busy and could not take them to the match? What if the player cannot afford to play in competitions were scouts regularly attend? What if that player is from a remote area, and the family does not have the resources to showcase their talent? What if that player is participating in another football code and has technical skills beyond your belief transferable to our sport? What if that player wasn't feeling well and didn't perform well on that particular day? More importantly, what if the parents cannot afford the hefty fees to play football? Let's be frank about this: some clubs see junior development as a cash cow and rely on it to finance their clubs.

"So, you can see we operate in an imperfect system of probability and chance. Sometimes we get it right and find talent; however, most of the time, there is a plethora of talented players you miss. I call this the lost opportunity for talent identification."

Gunnar paused and reached for a black metal case the size of a shoebox. He swiped a security card the size of a Mastercard to unlock the case. The audience waited in anticipation.

"Ladies and gentlemen, I have in front of me a smart armband that is the most integral part of the PVI system.

It's made of flexible and shatterproof material supported by one of the smallest microprocessors available on the market. The player wears the device as a smart armband throughout the match. The player data—algorithms—is transmitted to our drone for collation and then analysed. It has no adverse effects on the health of the player, and, as you can see, it's the size of a small watch."

The image of the smart armband projected onto the big screen in three-dimensional imagery. Gunnar demonstrated the armband by clipping it to his right arm. It attached firmly and locked onto his arm without any issues.

"See how easy that was to attach to my arm? If you look on the screen, I will demonstrate the signal strength of the device to transmit data."

I can't believe this is happening before me, Robby thought.

As Gunnar shuffled around, making a variety of hand and foot movements to simulate a football player, the data started scrolling on the screen. It was capturing all the relevant player movements. Samples of data regarding agility, strength, prowess, decision-making, creativity, and acceleration filtered across the big screen. Red, green, and blue bar graphs appeared. Every time he moved a part of his body, the armband captured the data.

What does all this data mean, and how is it analysed? Robby thought. He was becoming even more inquisitive.

Gunnar stopped moving around, removed the armband, and switched it off.

"Now, let's process our data against the player profiles we have developed in our system. You will note a ranking of player potential for my movements." He placed the armband on the table and patiently waited.

A score of 2 out of 10 flashed across the screen. The patrons in the room looked surprised and didn't know what to think of it.

"As you can see, I will never make it as a footballer!" Gunnar said. The audience chuckled.

"Ladies and gentlemen, tomorrow you are all invited for a one-hour bus trip to the picturesque town of Keflavík to witness the PVI system live in action. There will be a scheduled simulation with the local football club and their junior development squad. The club is Keflavík ÍF, and you are all welcome to attend. If you could please advise us of your attendance by midday today, we will book your seat on the bus. It will be your opportunity to review the system and ask lots of questions.

"There is also a special surprise tomorrow. I will be launching the drone Mark II to collate player algorithms and send it back to our computers for analysis. I will ask you all to sign a confidentiality agreement, as the drone is in beta testing and you will be the first people to see it outside of Iceland. I wish to remind you this project is sensitive, and no one will be allowed on the bus without their security pass. You will not be allowed to use your cameras and recording devices at the venue. Security personnel will be present to ensure there is no breach of our rules."

Robby was captivated by what he had seen and was keen to book his spot on the bus trip straight away. Visiting Keflavík wasn't on his itinerary, and its mention came as a surprise. All journeys have their unexpected encounters, and he had visited faraway places before not knowing what to expect. It was an opportunity to get to know the culture, the country, and the people as much as the PVI system. He had many questions about what he had witnessed, and he would use the afternoon to write a list of observations.

However, there was going to be a problem in attending the tour in Keflavík, and his emotions about the new technology were controlling his rational thinking. His flight was scheduled for the next morning, and he was required to be back at work immediately upon his return. His boss was unforgiving, and a pile of work was building day by day. There were essential meetings already scheduled in Sydney with agents to finalise multimillion-dollar player contracts. A no-show could put his job on the line.

Being able to visit and see the PVI system firsthand was a chance of a lifetime, and it was unlikely he would get back to Reykjavík shortly. He faced a dilemma: pack up and leave the next day, therefore missing out on assessing the revolutionary technology, or lose his job. He had to make a decision quickly.

Before leaving the auditorium for his hotel room next to the foyer, Robby made sure he registered his name for the field trip to Keflavik. The short walk up the escalator leading to his room was just enough for him to ponder about the next day.

He paced anxiously in his hotel room. If one didn't know about his dilemma, that person would have thought he was going mad.

Oh, God, what do I do? he thought.

2 | A Day at Keflavík FC

Teams don't learn. Individuals within the team learn. Development is a personal process, even when conducted in a team environment.

Johan Cruyff, football legend

It was a chilly morning in Reykjavík, and the wind had a bitter bite to it. Perhaps Gunnar had been right when he had sarcastically made a joke about the temperament of the Icelandic climate. His track jacket wasn't going to be enough to keep him warm. Robby had thought he could tough it out as an icy cold breeze lashed across his forehead and receding hairline. His three-day beard growth wasn't much help either. It was a reminder that he wasn't as tough as he thought he was. He realised this was no time for being a champion, and he put on his beanie and padded training jacket.

Two buses had parked at the front of the hotel while the patrons were queuing to be seated. It seemed everyone that had attended the conference was coming for the ride. One by one, they handed over their signed confidentiality agreements before boarding the thirty-seater bus. The same security guards from the day before stood next to each bus monitoring the patrons and checking passes before they boarded.

Robby could hear noises coming from the door of the second bus. He turned around to find two security guards questioning an Asian man.

"Where is your pass?" one security guard asked. "You can't board the bus without a pass."

The man spoke broken English, insisting he was legitimate and tried to board anyway.

"Stop, sir, or I will have to apprehend you. Do not enter the bus."

"Bié pèng wǒ! Bié pèng wǒ!" Do not touch me, he said in Chinese.

Although the security guards politely tried to stop the man from boarding the bus, it descended into pushing and shoving. He wasn't cooperating with them.

"Bié pèng wǒ! Bié pèng wǒ!" The Chinese man was becoming very agitated.

One of the security guards grabbed the man by the arm, twisted it, and apprehended him as the other guard escorted him to the hotel foyer. Nobody knew who this person was and why he had tried to board. He had not been present at the seminar yesterday and looked as though he had other motives, having appeared from nowhere and lacking a valid pass to show his credentials.

All of this for a new technology based on player identification? Robby thought. It didn't make any sense: the tight security, the checks for identification. There was more to it, and it felt suspicious.

The Chinese man was persistent. "Fàng kāi wǒ!' "Let me go," he said in Chinese.

He could see Liam behind him in the queue. Liam pointed to the bus he was boarding, suggesting they could sit together. He understood what Liam was on about and nodded more than once to confirm. As he boarded the bus to take his seat next to Liam, he could hear police sirens in the distance. It was a serious matter for the Icelandic people, and he started to piece the puzzle together.

"You know, I was thinking about this last night," Robby said.

"Oh yes, yesterday's presentation did give us much to think about." Liam looked towards him. "What's on your mind?"

"I often have thought about the nations that consistently dominate world football and why."

"That's a complex question," Liam said.

"Is it because they have a culture of football, lots of money to spend on developing their talent, and a big population?"

"It's a question I often have asked myself."

"Perhaps world football domination is led by nations that can harness smart technology to identify talent from a limited catchment of players?"

"I see where you are coming from," Liam said, acknowledging the breadth of discussion, and he was interested.

"Look at Iceland, with a limited population, rugged landscape, and its isolation. A lack of football resources compared with other nations, and yet they continue to outperform in the world rankings. Consistently punching above their weight to everyone's surprise."

"I guess that's why we are here." Liam paused as he adjusted his seat belt. "I am sure we will find out soon what makes this tiny nation click on the world football stage."

"So, what do you know about Keflavík football club?"

"I have a leaflet I got from the hotel yesterday. Let me read it to you." Liam pulled out a brochure from his pocket and unfolded it. "Keflavík won its first title in 1964. The team also won the titles in 1969, 1971, and 1973. Since then, they have mostly played in Iceland's top division, Úrvalsdeild. The team is now playing the Icelandic Premier League."

"You always have been resourceful." Robby was not

surprised that he had done his homework. That was what made him a successful scout.

They both sat back in their seats and peered outside the window. They were on the outskirts of Reykjavík as the bus continued on the semi-barren coastal drive to Keflavík. Trees along the roadside transformed into a sea of volcanic rock ashes. Green moss clung to the craggy outcrops. Tiny droplets of rain saturated the windows. It was a typical Icelandic day.

Robby decided to search the internet about the Keflavík football club. He wanted to know more. He read from Wikipedia about the club's origins.

Keflavík ÍF is an Icelandic sports club, from the town of Reykjanesbær. The club has several divisions for different sports: football, basketball, swimming, gymnastics, badminton, shooting, and taekwondo. Its most significant divisions are Knattspyrnudeild Keflavíkur (football) and Körfuknattleiksdeild Keflavíkur (basketball) . . . Keflavík Youth Club (Ungmennafélag Keflavíkur, UFMK) was founded on 29 September 1929 by twenty-eight young people in the town of Keflavík. The club became a member of The Icelandic Youth Federation, which had been established in 1907 as part of Icelana's drive for independence.

Keflavík was the perfect backdrop for demonstrating the PVI system. It was only an hour's drive from Reykjavík. The club had a professional junior development program for residents of the local area with an extensive catchment of players to identify talent. It was synonymous for youth development, as its history would suggest, developing great talent over the years.

The stadium was compact and built to cater to a loyal supporter base of around 5,000 people. It had manicured training pitches and all the facilities one would expect from a club with such a long history and presence in the Icelandic top tier. It was the perfect alliance for Gunnar and his team of experts to fine-tune his player identification system.

Gunnar stood up at the front of the bus. The driver handed him a wireless microphone.

"Dear friends, I thought while travelling to Keflavík football club that I explain to you all a little more about Icelandic football." He adjusted the volume on the microphone settings. "Ah, I think it's better . . . can you all hear me now?" He continued talking while balancing himself against the movements of the bus. "Football in Iceland has transformed over the decades with better infrastructure and playing facilities. The Icelandic Football Federation constructed dynamic artificial turf that is temperature-controlled to ensure an optimum playing surface. Indoor playing became the benchmark for our training standards. Players could develop in an environment that was stable and not subject to the icy winds and subzero winters."

"When did this all change?" a patron asked.

"That's a good question." Gunnar thought about his response. "At least twenty years ago after a strategic football conference held by the Icelandic Football Federation. Football in Iceland is not a summer sport like before, limited to four months of the year. Leading this development was Keflavík ÍF, and it has become the hub for the Icelandic talent development program."

"So is that why we are going there today?" another patron asked.

"Yes, it's a strategic alliance co-opted by the Icelandic Football Federation and my team to develop new footballing talent with innovative technologies. This new technology is now ready for the world to see. Today, it will be showcased for the first time to invited representatives from football federations outside of Iceland like you."

The bus arrived at the home of Keflavík ÍF, and the blue-and-white colours of the club were visible at the main entrance of the stadium. As they stepped off the bus and back into the cold temperatures, a gust of cold wind sent a chilling reminder through their bones. They all made their way to the staging area inside the stadium.

Robby took his seat in the undercover section with all the patrons. He was carefully acknowledging what was happening in front of him. There was commotion around the staging area, where at least eighty teenagers were lined up into groups.

Gunnar's technical assistant stood up in front of them and asked for their attention. "I would like to explain what is happening in the staging area."

He paused and waited for the patrons to settle in their seats. Then he said, "The players are fitting their armbands and registering their signature codes so we can use the algorithms to measure their performances. That requires scanning the armbands with a laser detection device and then recording the players' names in the system. Every staging area has a computer hub and signal devices that resemble antennas. Every player has a unique code associated with their profile. After the registration is complete, the players will move to a second staging post to double-check their devices and reaffirm their details. It was important that every player was identified in the PVI system to ensure there was an accurate assessment."

The technical assistant took a deep breath and continued. "From the second staging area, players will move into their various teams for twenty-minute round-robin matches."

Robby was fascinated and enthralled by the organisation and technology.

"Not every player will play on the same team. The data is analysed in real-time after each round of matches, and the system will recommend changes to player positions for the next round of matches. There is no ranking. It's important that all players have an equal opportunity to perform. The only changes players experience is positional and matchups against others with different attributes."

The technical assistant finished his commentary and made his way to the staging area. Gunnar called the patrons to attention. He was excited to demonstrate his system.

"I welcome you again, and it's great to see an excellent response to our field trip. What you see today is the Player Virtual Identification process that's been implemented in Iceland for the past two years. We have refined it and made it better over time. So let me explain . . ."

A silence descended over the group.

"We have invited eighty players from the local community, which also includes exclusive representation from players based on the east coast of Iceland. They have been randomly allocated teams." Gunnar took a sip from his bottle of water and rested his right arm on the handrail.

"The PVI system and the assessment process do not end here. There are selected players that will retain their armbands and take them back to their local competitions so we can continue assessing their performance."

Gunnar then raised his right hand to communicate an important point. "One of the flaws of traditional player identification is that it's usually a one-off assessment process. Players are prematurely cut from the list and sometimes for the wrong reasons. What if a player needs further assessment because you need to validate their attributes in a certain area? And what if they show elements of brilliance and you want to verify it for consistency?"

I wonder what he's leading up to, Robby thought.

"Identifying football talent is a subjective process based on the opinion of a few people, and sometimes it has unconscious bias." He paused again to take a deep breath. "You may like a player for reasons that only satisfy your perception. That is your expectation of a talented player in terms of their skill and attributes. But that is the flawed process, and our system eliminates that unconscious bias."

"What do you mean by that? Can you expand on that point?" a patron asked.

"That is a good question. Let me explain." He looked towards the patron with piercing eyes. "You may prefer the profile of a centre forward that is tall, has body strength, and excellent heading abilities. But what if I presented a player that could play in that position that didn't have all these physical attributes? Would you be interested in that player?"

There was dead silence. No one had an answer to the question.

"I have found such a player in Iceland that could be atypical of a centre forward, and he is now playing in the under 20 national team."

"Can we see the drone?" another patron asked.

"Yes. Of course, that's what you came here to see. If you are all ready, let's walk down to pitch level." Gunnar stalled for a moment while touching his forehead. "Oh, that reminds me . . . what happened today while boarding the bus was nothing to be concerned about."

"Why was he taken away?" a patron asked.

"He wasn't a guest, and he tried to board the bus with fake identification. We have had situations where other countries have tried to steal our intellectual property because we refuse to sell it to them. They are concerned about our rapid development in world football. You know, these things can become political."

"Did you find out who this person was?" another patron asked.

Gunnar took his time before answering. "I am not sure

I can go into that because it's with our police. They are looking into it."

Gunnar waved to all the patrons and asked them to follow him to ground level to see the drone in operation.

Like a group of schoolchildren eagerly waiting to enter a fairground attraction, all the patrons picked up their bags and gingerly followed him, jostling to maintain their spot in the queue. Robby was unfazed and prepared to wait his turn as he followed the full line of enthusiasts. It was orderly, but everyone had an underlying intent to get in first.

As the queue passed the first level of the stadium, they could see the trial matches in full swing on the main pitch. It was a six-to-a-side game in a condensed pitch size to accentuate the skills associated with quick movement and thinking. Robby noticed each player had the armband securely fastened to their upper arm. Yellow-and-greens lights flickered at high speed as the communication device sent data to the computer hub.

I can't believe this is all happening in front of me, he thought. *We are in the dark ages in comparison back home.*

The patrons followed Gunnar to a room behind a large glass window adjacent to the halfway line of the pitch. They all trotted in one by one in a straight line. They saw large monitor screens and half a dozen analysts sorting through the data to establish patterns of performance. Every player had a number, and each name had bar graphs that continuously changed shape as the data rolled in. More importantly, one big screen only showed three numbers, which indicated a player had reached the performance criteria set by the system. These were the talented players that the system had flagged them for further assessment based on their potential.

"Come around, my dear friends," Gunnar called enthusiastically. "Let me show you the heart of our system . . . the assessment room." He pointed to a series of computers and screens in front of the patrons. "These guys are my technical assessors, and their job is to collate the data and come up with player profiles that look promising in the early stages. As you can see on the big screen in front of you, so far, we have identified three talented players this morning. I will be looking at these profiles with interest later on."

There was a slight murmur in the room as the patrons nodded and sighed in disbelief. It was the space odyssey of football talent identification. It was a look into the future when it came to unlocking talent and potential and a masterful achievement built by a genius that would change the dynamics of world football domination.

"Now, please step outside to see we all have been

waiting for." Gunnar's tone had a boyish lilt. "I want you all to look above the halfway line, and you will see a drone hovering above you." He pointed above so everyone could see. "There you have it . . . our football drone is collating data and transmitting to our assessment centre."

The drone buzzed ahead like an overgrown pollinating bee. It appeared sturdy, securely holding its elevation despite a slight breeze blowing against it. Considering its size—it was the length of a motorbike—it had remarkable directional control.

As the trial game came to an end, the drone moved over to the other side of the pitch to follow another match that had commenced. One could not help but notice the awe in the players as they instinctively looked above to see it flying into position. They liked the drone as much as the trial matches. The family and friends of the players seated in the front rows of the stadium also were enthralled. Some of the parents had travelled from the other side of the island to participate in the trial. They pointed to the drone as though it were a carnival sideshow.

I wonder how far it can travel to assess players . . . 100, 200 kilometres? Who knows? Robby thought.

Gunnar informed the patrons that the drone was an innovative invention and the next step in the development of the PVI system. It could be sent to remote areas and stream data back to the assessment centre. It was the virtual talent scout that could travel to locations that were difficult to reach because of their remoteness; a "go anywhere" player discovery unit that could capture a much wider talent pool.

For example, a player in the remote area of the Brazilian interior could become discoverable. All he had to do was wear the armband and participate in an organised trial with his local football federation. Or perhaps an African boy who lacked the financial means to play football could be issued an armband by his local school and assessed during interschool matches.

Whatever the place, circumstance, or socioeconomic background of the individual, every boy—or girl—had a shot at being identified. The only common denominator was talent and a natural ability to outperform in football. If someone had the talent, then the system would find them, and from there on, who knows what changes to their life this would bring? Perhaps an opportunity for a shot at the big time?

During the drone demonstration, Robby was standing close to the control unit that the ground pilot used. It contained the details of the company that had developed it. He was sharp and never missed an opportunity to find out more. That was why he was such a good talent scout.

He paid attention to detail, and the ability to see things that others missed altogether was a key strength. He wrote down *PDI (Player Discovery Incorporated)* and noted the "Made in Iceland" symbol below where it was written on the control unit.

While everyone had taken off for a coffee break, he accessed the internet to find out about the company. PDI had an office on the outskirts of Reykjavík in an old industrial estate. He had no intention of going home until he visited the company to find out more about the technology and its potential use outside of Iceland. It could put him one step ahead of his colleagues and the other football federations around the world.

He read the home page of the company on the internet with great interest. PDI was a start-up company between two football enthusiasts with engineering and communication backgrounds. The company had commenced five years ago with humble beginnings with one prototype drone. Since then, they had advanced their technology to the next-generation model and named it the Spatial Awareness Drone-Mark II. It was a much stronger and robust drone that had undergone testing in several rugged environments to assess its capacity to deliver information from remote locations. An essential part of the testing was the ability for the drone to work in different climatic conditions, travel longer distances, and hover above playing fields for long periods. Not an easy feat and essential for the delivery and integrity of the data on player performance.

The demonstration concluded after thirty minutes, and Gunnar thanked everyone for their interest and attendance. After the event, the patrons took advantage of their location and made arrangements to depart from Keflavík International Airport on that same day. It was only five minutes by taxi or bus, and there was no need to return to Reykjavík. They all said their goodbyes to one another and hailed cabs for the short drive to the airport.

It was difficult to gauge whether the Icelandic climate had taken its toll on the patrons or whether they had enjoyed their experience. All except Robby, who had plans of this own. The demonstration of the PVI system wasn't enough. He wanted to know more, and the drone, in particular, had captured his imagination. Coming from Australia, a country of vast distances and rugged landscapes, getting to remote areas was not feasible for talent scouts. He could see how the drone would provide significant benefits to identifying talent in Outback Australia.

3 | The Football Engineer

OK, the wonderful thing about soccer is, a football is a perfectly round object, and it doesn't make mistakes. The player using it makes mistakes. And the more you use it, the fewer mistakes you make.

Craig Johnston, Australian football legend

Robby stepped into the taxi queue and waited his turn. A slate-grey Volkswagen pulled up alongside him as the driver waved him in. He asked the driver to take him to the registered address of PDI.

"Are you sure you want to go there, sir?" the taxi driver asked. He spoke rudimentary English.

"Yes, it's the right address."

"Sir, it's an industrial place. I have never taken a tourist there." The driver was bemused and making sure Robby was certain about his destination.

"Oh, yes. It's correct. I contacted the company this morning to check, and it's the right place."

The driver was satisfied; Robby appeared confident where he was going. "OK, sir, step in, and I can take you there."

The taxi briskly took off to Reykjavík. This time, Robby was intent on more intuitively soaking in the surroundings, as the weather had cleared. The drive was more interesting this time as he took note of the developing infrastructure in the gateway between Reykjavík and Keflavík. The Icelandic economy was modern and developing. A new port and shopping precincts were visible from the road. However, in the Icelandic capital, football fields were not a common sight, unlike in his native country. Gunnar had commented about the harsh climate in winter and football's transition to indoor facilities. It began to make sense.

"We are a few minutes away, sir," the driver said.

"Thank you." He was pleased to have reached his destination.

"What about going back, sir?" The driver paused for a moment. "Do you need a ride back?" His Icelandic accent made it hard to understand.

Robby thought for a moment. He had never pondered how he was going to get back to the hotel. "I think that would be great. I will be here for at least one hour."

"So at three p.m., sir?"

"Yes, I think that will give me plenty of time."

"Here is my card with my phone number. And here we

are, sir. Player Discovery Incorporated over there."

He stepped out of the cab and thanked the driver. "See you in an hour, then."

The estate was industrial and a mixture of old and new buildings. On the other side of the road was a series of decaying timber structures that had seen better days. They were falling apart, and the rotten frames supporting the rusted ceilings were slanting to one side. The road leading to the drone manufacturer was a series of potholes the taxi driver navigated to avoid undercarriage damage.

The building housing PDI was uncharacteristically modern with a large driveway and roller door entrance. A sign directing all visitors to reception provided reassurance this was a professional business and not a two-bit operation. As he made his way to the main entrance, Robby could not help but peek into a small opening in the garage door. Two technicians in high-visibility uniforms were fussing around a drone. Large machines were plugged into it.

It's pretty high-tech, he thought.

He pressed the doorbell, waited for several minutes, and tried again.

A security guard entered the reception area: a towering, muscly man with short blond hair. His sculptured face and broad shoulders made him an imposing figure. Robby wondered why a business in a rundown industrial estate would need a security guard.

"Can I help you, sir?" the security guard asked in a heavy Icelandic accent.

"Yes, I am looking for Gunnar Grimsson."

"And who may you be?"

"I'm Robby Denehy from the Australian Football Federation, and I'm in Iceland for a football seminar that Gunnar presented."

"Does he know you're coming to see him?"

"Well . . . not really. I thought while I was in Reykjavík, it might be a good time to meet him before I leave tonight."

"Your name is Robby, right?"

"Yes."

The security guard crossed his arms and looked him directly in the eye, nodding his head a few times.

"Will it be possible to speak to him?"

"Hmm . . . wait here, and I will see him and come back to you."

At least fifteen minutes passed before the security guard returned with Gunnar by his side.

"Hello, I am Gunnar Grimsson. I don't think we have met before."

"Good morning, sir. I am Robby Denehy from the Australian Football Federation. I am a senior player scout."

"Ah . . . you're an Australian guy." Gunnar fiddled with his overgrown beard. "Oh yes, welcome, and please come inside. You have come a long way to see me."

He walked briskly, leading the way and pointing to a meeting room ahead. "Over here, Mr Denehy."

Robby took a seat in a room that looked like an operational control centre. Diagrams, drawings, objectives, and data were posted everywhere next to pictures of the drone. There were components laid across a desk that looked advanced in comparison to anything Robby had seen before.

"So, what brings you all this way to this unattractive part of Reykjavík?" Gunnar paused, then said, "I don't get many visitors here unless they are on a mission!"

"I want to understand more about the drone you have developed. I come from a country of vast distances and remote locations. It continues to be a source of frustration."

"Yes, I understand." Gunnar was very interested in his plight. "We have the same issue here in Iceland, and this is the main reason why I developed this technology."

Robby had an intense look in his eyes. "Can you tell me more?"

Gunnar jumped right into it and didn't mince his words. "There are two places I am trialling the advanced drone at the moment." He pointed to a large map of

Iceland on the wall behind him. "Akureyri is a town in northern Iceland, and it is Iceland's second-largest urban area, nicknamed the capital of North Iceland."

"Do you ever have issues with bad weather in that part of Iceland?"

"The area has a relatively mild climate because of geographical factors, and the town's ice-free harbour has its advantages."

"How many trials have you completed successfully in Akureyri?" Robby had trouble with his Icelandic pronunciation.

"It's been our third trial, and I have been able to receive data from a junior tournament 150 kilometres away.' Gunnar paused and grinned. "Oh, we did have to land the drone during a freak storm, but that was all part of the testing. It wasn't damaged, and we were pleased with that."

"That's amazing it could travel such a distance and return undamaged."

"Yes, the next-generation model, Mark II, was built to travel longer distances with greater reliability and send data in poor weather conditions." He was getting excited about his progress. "The farther we can travel into remote areas, the better our catchment of players, making the system more viable for our football federation."

"That is amazing!"

"For example, Húsavík is a town in the Norðurþing municipality on the north coast of Iceland. It's located on the shores of Skjálfandi Bay with 2,182 permanent inhabitants. Húsavík is also served by its airport, which helps us with the setup of the drone." Gunnar took a sip of coffee from a handmade Icelandic mug. "We completed a simulation flight last weekend and monitored the effects of the 150-kilometre flight."

"That's a long distance to travel."

"It's the longest flight so far, and the results from the data obtained is showing a lot of promise."

"I really must say how excited I am as a professional football scout by what you have developed here. I have never had the means to scout players in remote locations."

"It's a similar problem to Iceland," Gunnar said.

"Yes, very similar, and sometimes I wonder what talent is lurking out in places I have never been able to discover."

Gunnar smiled in appreciation. "I have found two talented players already in Akureyri that is being further assessed by the Icelandic Football Federation." He pulled out two photos from the top drawer. "A fifteen-year-old farmer's boy and a sixteen-year-old plumbing apprentice with amazing talent. I discovered them during a junior tournament three months ago."

"They are on your talent identification program now?"

"Yes, these two boys are in Reykjavík working with our talent identification coach. There was no way I would ever have found them through the traditional scouting process."

Robby wanted to know more. "I assume when you discover a talented player, you hand over the data to the Icelandic Football Federation?"

"Yes. The Federation has full rights to the data and the player once they are deemed to be at the standard required for the development program." Gunnar smiled. "It's part of the deal: we operate and support the system under a license agreement."

"Any licensing arrangements overseas?"

"Not at this stage. Our licensing arrangement with the Icelandic Football Federation has a restriction on selling this technology in Europe. I am considering licensing this technology outside of Europe because Iceland does not face off with those countries at any level of competition."

"Can I ask a question about the security around this new technology?"

Gunnar laughed. "I see you have met our security guards."

"Oh, more than once, and I don't think it's a coincidence." Robby was sarcastic.

"I don't let anyone see my technology. It's too vital to our football federation. It's an integral part of their strategy to become a world football power."

"I can see it's taken very seriously in Iceland."

"The security is necessary to stop intellectual theft of our technology." Gunnar lowered his tone to a whisper. "We had Chinese operatives try to infiltrate our computers and steal our designs."

"I wasn't aware you had these issues, but I can understand why other countries would want to get a hand on your technology." Robby was beginning to appreciate the sensitivities around this innovative system.

"We are ranked in the top ten in the world with a small population. It all happened very quickly over five years, and other football superpowers are curious."

"I understand the security presence now."

"Yes. For some countries, football is political and, particularly where it's the number one national sport, it's like a religion. We had a security breach at the hotel today and apprehended a person with a fake visa." Gunnar appeared to know all about the kerfuffle.

"Well, I was there, and I saw it . . . and I must say I had no idea what was going on."

"You are the only representative from a football federation outside of Iceland to take the initiative to inquire about the drone," Gunnar said.

"Was it because other countries were not aware of their

potential? Maybe they found it too farfetched or ahead of its time?"

"You know, football does not stay the same. It evolves, and we find new ways of discovering talent. It's about creating an environment where everyone can participate and have an opportunity to showcase themselves. Most will never make it. But every once in a while, something special comes along out of nowhere that makes the whole profession of talent identification so exciting."

"I couldn't agree more. I have felt this feeling before," Robby said.

Gunnar asked if he was interested in taking a walk through the technical department to see the current prototype drone. It only took him a split second to agree.

They briskly put on white dust coats and caps.

"Tell me why you got started in this development. You left a good job to pursue this interest?" Robby asked.

"My story is one that thousands of parents could tell you, and it lies at the core problem of player identification." Gunnar opened the security door to the workshop. "My son was a very talented sixteen-year-old with tremendous potential. I was scheduled to take him for a trial in Reykjavík from our village 100 kilometres away when I got caught in a storm."

"I'm assuming you ended up never taking him."

"That's right, and because it was the only day the trial was scheduled in Reykjavík, he missed out."

"There was no exemption or a new trial date for your son?" Robby could see where this discussion was heading.

"No. My son wasn't the only one affected on this occasion. I could think of at least twenty other players in the same situation." Gunnar's eyes cringed.

"So, disappointment led to your idea?"

"My colleague and I met one night and talked about it and, being engineers; we started thinking outside the box."

"What happened then?"

"We used a napkin to draw a prototype drone and discussed the concept." Gunnar's face lit up. "I think the Icelandic beer also helped that night!"

They both smiled as they arrived at the cleanroom and changed into white disposable shoes to avoid any contamination. The drone was in front of them. It sat next to the previous model.

"It's sturdier and more technologically advanced than the previous version," Gunnar said. He took a deep breath. "It's fitted with high-tech lenses for video monitoring and antennas as part of the high-tech communication module. It's propelled by electrical power generated by a series of sophisticated batteries."

"That's incredible!"

"The drone has a twelve-hour battery life when in flight mode, which can be extended by solar receptors, depending on the weather. In sunlight, it can extend battery life to almost twenty-four hours. It made travelling longer distances possible."

"You know your stuff," Robby said.

"The done is powered by our trademark-designed engines built specifically to handle the turbulent Icelandic storms that lash the island without warning. Powerful pulse engines with automatic stabilisers mean it can withstand a storm with gusts up to 100 kilometres an hour and fierce rain." Gunnar was on a roll and enjoyed talking about the mechanical design.

"So it's sturdier than the previous model?"

"Yes, the onboard computer is the heart of the unit that manages every action of the drone."

"I'm so impressed." Robby could not hide his feelings about the technology. "I don't know what to say, other than you have opened opportunities to many young people."

"That brings me to my next point. Any licensing agreement is based on a commitment by the football federation of that country to genuinely use the unit to discover players that are out of reach and unable to attend talent identification assessments."

Robby had been waiting for this moment. "I understand why you would want these assurances."

"We ask for data sharing to ensure the information is used with the same principles in mind." Gunnar pointed to a large whiteboard with pictures of successful players that the player discovery system had found.

"You have had several successes, I can see."

Gunnar was delighted and ready to show off his exploits. "Yes, five in total and all are playing for their respective age group at the international level for Iceland."

"I wish I had more time to talk about your system."

"Well, you are always welcome back tomorrow for coffee and to continue talking." Gunnar also enjoyed his company. "I don't always talk to people like this. My friends find me a little reclusive and hard to approach sometimes."

"I appreciate your welcoming me today, and I guess I am in a fortunate position to experience what's happening here." Robby paused to think about his next move. If he were going to leave, it would have to be now. His flight was departing in three hours. He also had to wrestle with his demanding employer back home. How would this impact his job if he didn't arrive back at work on time?

Thoughts kept racing through his mind. *Should I? Shouldn't I? Do I take a risk?*

"Well, what do you say? See you tomorrow? You know, there's a lot more I haven't told you about," Gunnar said.

The taxi was waiting outside and honking to announce its arrival. He had to get back to the hotel in enough time to gather his belongings and leave for Keflavík International Airport. He had to make a decision and quickly.

Robby wasn't going to get anywhere with a single chat if he wanted Gunnar's confidence and trust. He needed to build a relationship if he had any hope of securing a license agreement from him.

He faced a personal dilemma. The technology was the chance of a lifetime and everything he had dreamed. However, it could come at the expense of his steady job.

Robby's meeting with Gunnar in Iceland didn't end as many would have predicted, and he missed his flight from Reykjavík that afternoon. He extended his stay for another week to learn more about the PVI system to the annoyance of his employer. It nearly cost him his job. However, he wrote a short report summarising the benefits of the PVI system to his boss that managed to tweak his interest.

During this time, he got to understand Gunnar much better and appreciate his scouting and player development philosophy. The knowledge gained by him was vital to building an enduring relationship with Gunnar and reach agreement on a consulting arrangement with the Australia Football Federation.

Gunnar had never before entertained an international football federation outside of Iceland, mainly due to his philosophy on developing and accessing young talent. He had some strong views about the use of the system and how football federations should implement it. This philosophy didn't go down well with his colleagues in mainland Europe.

Robby understood what the PVI system was meant to do. There was a sense of community and benevolence about his views. It was about developing and providing an opportunity to those that didn't have parents with fat cheque books and connections as a means of gaining opportunity. Because football is about finding talent where you least expect it; Diego Maradona, Pele, George Best, David Beckham, to mention a few.

Robby's new objective was to discuss the potential implementation of the PVI system in Australia with Gunnar.

He was impressed by Robby's passion and the stories of outback Australia and the indigenous people. The vast countryside meant that many young players missed out on the same opportunities afforded to the city kids. In many ways, it was a similar tale to the Icelandic experience.

4 | The Desert Rose

It's time we stopped talking about qualifying for the World Cup and started talking about winning it.

Johnny Warren, soccer legend

Gunnar was at the Football Federation Australia headquarters in Sydney, the venue for the meeting of key stakeholders. He stood awkwardly in front of the delegates, fidgeting from one leg to another to find an appropriate pose. It was an unusual stance, but Gunnar wasn't your typical person. He was conscious of his presentation and could not find the right position with confidence to commence his discussion. He stood up and filled his glass with water to calm his nerves. It appeared to work, as he covered his mouth and cleared his throat in anticipation. He was ready to unleash his speech about his invention to the anxious delegates waiting to hear what he had to say.

Six months earlier and during his extended week in Iceland, Robby got to understand Gunnar better and appreciate his scouting and player development philosophy. The knowledge he had gained was key to building an enduring relationship with Gunnar and reaching an agreement on a consulting arrangement with the Australia Football Federation.

"Dear delegates," Gunnar said, "if you had asked me ten years ago that I would be presenting my player identification system to a group of important football people in a country on the other side of the world, I would have grinned and said, 'You are dreaming.'"

The delegates chuckled at Gunnar's sense of humour.

"However, I want to first share my story with you and why a communications engineer like myself, with an innate passion for football, decided to dedicate their entire life to designing and developing the PVI system.

"The principle that underpins the foundation of the system is about fairness. Every football player has a right to showcase their talent if they feel motivated to do so. That does not mean they have a right to play in the English Premier League, for example, for that is about performance. However, the right to have an opportunity for a professional football career is something that every passionate football player can dream about."

Robby could see the interest that Gunnar's opening words generated in the room, and you hear could hear a pin drop. It was Robby that convinced his boss to organise the presentation to key stakeholders' when he arrived from

Iceland. As the presentation organiser, he was proud of the response from the delegates and their keen interest.

"Let's be frank: football talent identification is far from perfect, and the system has been designed in a way so that talent scouts will only discover a small sample of football players. What if your parents live in a remote area and don't have the means to play football regularly? What if your parents don't have the economic means to take their children training and pay the hefty association fees to play in a regular competition? What if your parents are not football fans, and the opportunity to be exposed to football is non-existent? I could go on and on with examples why the current system probably misses out on more talented players than it discovers."

There was a murmur in the room as the delegates gathered their thoughts and looked at one another with raised eyebrows.

"It happened to my son and his friends . . ." Gunnar paused to gather his thoughts. "My son is a talented football player, and I recognised this at an early age. There was a tournament in the capital of Reykjavík for players from our district in Iceland, which is a 100-kilometre distance on the northern tip of the island. A group of parents agreed to hire a minibus and drive to the tournament to showcase our talent in the area. As we were preparing our departure, a severe weather warning meant I had to cancel the journey.

"That was it: no trial and no other opportunity in the foreseeable future to participate as such events. The Icelandic Football Federation did not frequently organise trials in Reykjavík due to lack of resources and an unpredictable climate. Only the local boys from the capital and nearby districts were able to attend. The severe weather warning affected other families in other communities across Iceland. We were not the only ones that missed out.

"This is the football travesty I often speak about when describing what motivated me to develop this system. As a communication engineer, I partnered with a colleague who is an excellent software programmer to develop a system that could identify players in all remote locations. It could perform assessments over some time to obtain reliable data for talent identification."

He clicked over to a new slide with a summary in layman's terms of how the PVI operated.

"Delegates, the PVI system uses motion sensors from the smart armband and algorithms. This device tracks all the technical, tactical, biomechanical, and physical player movements on and off the ball. After five years of trials, I have developed the largest database of football movements in the world. I can identify talent quickly by profiling against our database. We know what exceptional talent looks like."

He sipped on a glass of water, then said, "On the table in front of you is the spatial-awareness drone. We use the term 'spatial awareness' because it can assess the movement of players under numerous settings and the game plays by hovering above a football field with the full pitch in view. It can profile decision-making and strategic play." Gunnar pointed directly to the drone with his index finger. "This drone is the antithesis of everything we do wrong today, and it is the future of football identification.

"Let me tell you the story of George Best and how Manchester United scout Bob Bishop discovered him in 1961 at the age of fifteen. He was captivated by George's raw talent. He sent Manchester United club manager Matt Busby a seven-worded telegram. The message read, 'I think I've found you a genius' . . . and the rest is history. If their paths hadn't intertwined, the world might never have known about George Best.

"George Best was undoubtedly the most naturally gifted British player of his generation. A combination of lightning pace, perfect balance, and ability to produce goals with both feet meant Best was a handful for defenders. What if Busby had not spotted him playing in the Belfast streets? It was only chance that Busby was able to come across such a remarkable talent. The world may never have known about George Best if Manchester City had not hired Busby to scour the Belfast playing fields for talented players."

Gunnar sipped his water again and continued. "However, George Best had a small frame for his age, and his physical appearance may have been deceiving to many talent scouts. His technical ability might have gone unnoticed if it wasn't for Busby's scouting abilities and his philosophy regarding the technical aptitude in a player." Gunnar paused again to get his thoughts together. "Do you all know the story of Johan Cruyff and how he was discovered?" he asked.

Everyone around the room looked at him and nodded.

"Johan Cruyff was ten years old when he was spotted by Jany van der Veen in the Netherlands. Jany said, 'Cruyff didn't need a discoverer, only someone who arranged his affairs. He was a godsend.'"

"The story of how he found Cruyff is very special. Jany always peeked out of his window, where he would often observe Johan Cruyff taking on the bigger kids. Such was his talent from a young age that he put him straight into the club at Ajax Amsterdam, rather than go through the usual process of a trial. Jany recalled Cruyff's intelligence in a simple manner: 'He always played football with the older boys, and he bossed them. It seemed like he was fused with the ball.'"

"Again, I wish to point out, what if Jany van der Veen wasn't looking out his window? And what if Johan Cruyff played elsewhere where he wasn't so visible to Jany? Whatever the case, this is an example where good luck, fortune, and talent seem to meet together at the right time and place."

Gunnar took a deep breath. "I suppose you all know how Lionel Messi was discovered? Carles Rexach discovered Messi at the age of thirteen and offered him the chance to train at football powerhouse FC Barcelona's youth academy, La Masia. Messi's family picked up and moved across the Atlantic to make a new home in Spain. The discovery of this talent had much to do with Messi requiring hormone treatment for a medical condition he had had since early childhood. It was during his time at Newell's Old Boys that his father sought help to cover the medical bills from the club.

"At that time, Messi had been noted for his extradentary talent, and the link with Barcelona and Carles Rexach started to be forged. The story of Lionel Messi and his discovery has as much to do with hormone treatment as it does about his extraordinary talent."

The delegates smiled and chuckled. They were fixed on his every word as the whole philosophy of the PVI system began to be revealed. Gunnar's personal experience had brought out the passionate side of his personality. It gave his presentation credibility in the eyes of the delegates.

"So, what will this system do for you? That is what you are here today to evaluate: the benefits of this system and what it may offer. The answer is simple, and it lies with your desert rose. A small, pink, five-petal flower with a red centre that gives it a stunning and unique contrast only found in remote areas of Australia. It appears from nowhere and in the most unexpected and inhospitable places. Finding the desert rose is not easy, and when you stumble onto it, you will admire its beauty. How can such a flower even grace such a harsh environment?

"Like the desert rose, how many footballers are out there waiting in places you would have never imagined unless you stumbled onto them? This system will help you find your desert rose and, who knows, perhaps the next superstar in your part of the world. On this basis, Robby has suggested we call this project 'the Desert Rose.' It is the foundation for finding something beautiful and extraordinary in places unexpected."

The delegates all stood up with a warm round of applause. They liked what they had heard from Gunnar's affectionate and passionate introduction.

"So there you have it. The Desert Rose," Robby said.

"The next part of our presentation is to demonstrate how the system will work." He looked around the room with a boyish grin. "Gunnar will now demonstrate the technology live from a location in Sydney. We have teamed up with a local club to run the demonstration."

To the surprise of the delegates, Robby had organised a trial match at the local football club in the Sydney suburb of Blacktown. He had used his connections to tap into the talent identification program that happened to be underway for players aged between fourteen and sixteen years. They had launched the drone above the football field to analyse the data live on the conference room screen. The delegates were going to see the PVI system in a live feed from the venue.

Meanwhile, Gunnar received an unusual text message on his phone from the technician at the venue.

"Hello, Gunnar, it's Magnus. We have a problem with the telecommunications link, and we aren't getting a data feed to the hub."

He took a deep breath while trying not to look too concerned. He responded by text: "We're presenting to the delegates in about fifteen minutes, and they are having a tea break. Do you think you can resolve it by then?"

"I don't know. I have grounded the drone and checked its communication microprocessor, and it's fine," Magnus replied. "I have checked the hub portal, and it's also working."

"OK."

"It might be something with the software, so I'm going to reboot the whole system and quickly get back to you."

"OK, Magnus. Message me back with an update."

It wasn't the first time there had been software issues with the PVI system, and usually, Magnus could repair it with a reboot, so Gunnar crossed his fingers in hope. He was concerned about presenting the PVI system to the delegates on time. They had been eagerly waiting to see the new technology on a live feed. A technical problem could send the wrong message altogether.

The delegates started making their way back from morning tea, albeit very slowly. Luckily for Gunnar, they were all in deep conversation and not in a hurry. His mobile phone rang, and Magnus appeared on the screen.

"Hi, Gunnar; it's me."

"How is it going?"

"The reboot appears to be working, and I'm getting live feed again."

"How much time do you need?" Gunnar asked.

"I'm preparing to relaunch the drone and reconnect the live feed with the hub." Magnus paused. "Can you give me another five minutes?"

"OK, Magnus. Get on it, and I will see what I can do here at my end.'

Not all the delegates had returned, and this provided Gunnar with an opportunity to stall his presentation for an extra few minutes. As with any meeting of like-minded professionals, tea breaks always represented an opportunity to talk about a range of other issues. Gunnar was banking on this to delay the presentation. He was confident Magnus would have things working again.

A text message with a big smiley face appeared on Gunnar's phone from Magnus, along with the word, "I'm nearly done!"

As the delegates took their seats, Gunnar could hear the sounds of pens clicking. There was the occasional look towards him. He took a deep breath, not knowing what to do next other than to stall for more time instinctively. He said, "Gentlemen, I am synchronising the link with our people on the ground and will be ready to go live soon."

Another message came from Magnus: "All good to go!"

Gunnar announced the next phase of the presentation without delay. He had avoided a total calamity and was keen to move on. Gunnar was a little red-faced, and sweat was forming above his eyebrows.

Another message came in from Magnus: "When you are finished, we need to discuss something extraordinary that happened today."

Gunnar was intrigued but had to push it aside for now. He said, "Delegates, here it is on the large screen . . . the live feed from Blacktown City FC."

Gunnar synced the remote with the projector and activated the data streaming. The data was being collected for each player during the trial match in Blacktown, profiling their capabilities. The trial had been underway for the last fifteen minutes, so the system was starting to analyse patterns of performance and produced green, blue, and red numbers with coloured bar graphs. The surnames and player portraits of top five performers were displayed. Numbers scrolled across the screen at rapid speed, representing key technical attributes. The PVI system also was matching with benchmark data previously attained from many years of testing in Iceland.

The power of the PVI system awed the delegates. Everyone's eyes focused on the monitor. Gunnar zoomed onto the players with the video feed from the drone. He wanted to show the smart armbands in operation. "Gentlemen, you can see the armbands fitted to the players that communicate with our drone," he said.

Several onlookers could be seen observing the drone manoeuvring across the pitch, and the delegates acknowledged the attention it created.

"I think we should have a quick break while I collate the findings of the data," Gunnar said.

The delegates nodded. It had been a great morning of information overload, and they needed time to absorb it.

"We are going to answer as many questions as possible when you all return." He looked around the room with a schoolboy's charm. "I will also profile a player that looks very promising from the data received so far. It's very encouraging."

The scene was set for an enthralling next chapter to the presentation. Magnus was doing a great job piloting the drone. Thanks to the organisation and cooperation of the players and coaches, everything was going to plan.

Gunnar stepped aside to speak to Robby to inform him what had occurred.

"Something happened at the venue," Gunnar said.

"I did notice a worried look on your face."

"Yes. Magnus would not have told me his concerns unless it's important."

He put down his pen and looked closer at the video link. "I did see someone unusual walking around the hub before the live feed commenced, but I made nothing of it."

"Really?" Gunnar said.

"I have seen this face before, but it won't come to me." He was trying to trace his thoughts back to Reykjavík.

"OK. If you have made a connection, let me know, and we can discuss it afterwards."

"Delegates, your attention please," Gunnar anxiously called. "I will now present to you our outstanding find from today's session based on our data analysis."

He clicked on the talent identification results, and a picture of a teenager of indigenous descent flashed across the screen. It was Harry Duwala from the Northern Territory and one of six players sponsored to trial as part of the indigenous pathway program to help support young people from the area. The program provided an opportunity to experience football. Harry stood out significantly from the other players. His scores were so high that the next-best player scored less than half of his performance.

Knowing he had made the perfect find; Gunnar had a cheeky grin on his face. He was going to take advantage and show off Harry Duwala to the delegates. More importantly, he was thrilled the player didn't come from the traditional pathways in Sydney. That was what the PVI system was meant to do: find the players that usually were off the radar.

Gunnar pointed to the profile of Harry. "What I like about Harry Duwala is he doesn't come through your traditional pathways for talent identification. He is an indigenous player from a community near Alice Springs. He is part of an indigenous pathway program that is supported by Blacktown City FC and the local government. I could be presumptuous and say he wasn't meant to be represented today if it wasn't for the indigenous program. He would not have been allowed to trial with other players from the local area in a coordinated program." Gunnar took a deep breath and paused. "Delegates, we have measured every player today against fourteen key criteria developed by the legendary Johan Cruyff. We have tested this criterion in Iceland for the last five years as the fundamental basis for identifying talent, and it works."

He pulled up a page on the screen showing the key criteria to help educate the delegates on the process of identification:

1. Team player: to accomplish things, you have to do them together.
2. Responsibility: take care of things as if they were your responsibility.
3. Respect: respect for one another.
4. Integration: involve others in your activities.
5. Initiative: dare to try something new.
6. Coaching: always help one another within a team.

7. Personality: be yourself.

8. Social involvement: interaction is crucial, both in sport and in life.

9. Technique: know the basics.

10. Tactics: know what to do.

11. Development: sport strengthens the body and soul.

12. Learning: try to learn something new every day.

13. Practice together: an essential part of any game.

14. Creativity: bring beauty to the sport.

Gunnar identified each criterion in detail and how the PVI system could measure against these elements through accurate data analysis, which was dependent upon recording player movements and decision-making during trial matches. Using a drone above the venue to measure player movement more accurately and record critical passages of play had improved analysis. It was a breakthrough in the system's design. The enhancements meant he could measure quality, technique, and vision differently. They were massive steps forward and a revolution in football talent identification.

By the end of Gunnar's presentation, the delegates were enthralled, except for one, who stood up and raised his concerns.

"I don't know about this technology," he said. "It all

looks like science fiction to me, and you have only used it in one small country." The delegate gazed around the room to get the attention of his colleagues. "Drones, algorithms, smart bands, computers . . . we are not Microsoft!"

There was an unnerving silence.

"We should give it a try," a delegate responded from across the table.

A debate broke out among the delegates about the benefits of the system. It went on for thirty minutes until they agreed to revisit the possibilities the next day. Everyone would be in limbo for the next twenty-four hours until they met again.

The objective of the presentation was to discuss the implementation of the PVI system in Australia and implement the test phase.

Later that afternoon, Robby and Gunnar met in the foyer to discuss how the day had gone.

"I'm glad it's finished," Gunnar said.

"It's been a big day. But we got through it, and we could have an agreement for one trial next month."

"Yes. That's positive. However, we are not out of the woods yet." Gunnar was concerned about the delegate from the city of Darwin and his capacity to sway the other delegates. He was chairman of the youth development committee and in charge of the football technical department. "We will find out tomorrow when they confirm whether to proceed or not."

Robby also was showing signs of strain in his voice. "Yes, it's unclear whether we will get the go-ahead for the trial." He paused. "You know, Gunnar, to think one delegate could derail everything we have strived for worries me."

"Politics, politics. It's everywhere, and football is no different." Gunnar smiled briefly. "He is an influential delegate, and it may derail us . . . but he is not the only decision-maker, and the others in the room were very keen on the technology."

"Yeah, maybe I am overreacting. Let's see how it goes tomorrow. I'm not going to jump to conclusions."

Gunnar patted him on the back. It was proving to be a difficult time for him, and he didn't like the situation.

"I'm sorry to bring you from Iceland and put you in a state of uncertainty. I thought it would have gone more smoothly today."

"It's not a problem; these things take time for people to adjust. We are changing the culture and the way football has been for a long time."

There was a brief silence as Robby soaked in the day's events. He was overthinking the whole presentation and not doing himself justice.

"Oh, I just remembered: I have something for you. I managed to get the pictures from the video feed," Robby said.

"Oh, have you found anything interesting?"

He pointed to his computer screen. "See this person . . . the Asian guy?"

"Yes, I can see his face standing next to the hub." Gunnar squinted and looked again. "But what is he doing so close to the hub?"

"Aha, well, he is the guy that pulled out the data cable."

"You're kidding!"

"Nope. That is the cable Magnus found disconnected. And you know what?"

"Tell me."

Robby had an intense look. "He was the guy at the Reykjavík hotel that was apprehended by security when I was boarding the bus."

"I can't believe this," Gunnar said. "He is a Chinese operative with fake documentation."

"Looks like he's back in business . . . and somehow he has found out we're in Sydney preparing another trial."

"So what do we do now?"

"We have more trials coming up to assess Harry Duwala in the next couple of days, and I might hire security at the venue."

"I agree. We need to make sure our technology is secure."

"Is it possible to find out more about him from the security people in Iceland?" Robby wanted to investigate further. "They took him away for questioning, and surely they built a profile on him."

"I can ask my contact at the Icelandic Football Federation and inform him what happened. They can release his identity so we can monitor for anything unusual during the next trial."

"I recall you telling me that other countries have tried to steal your technology before."

"Yes, but I didn't think they would come this far to Sydney." Gunnar was surprised. "It shows how important it is for them and the great lengths they will go to get a hold of my system."

"I'm starting to come to terms with it now."

"World football domination is what it comes down to," Gunnar said. "In some countries, football is politics, and national pride is at stake."

They commenced planning the security protocols for the next stage of the trials and arranged a meeting with a security firm the next day to shore up all contingencies. Nothing was going to be left to chance now that they had the evidence of subversive activity on video.

5 | My Name is Harry Duwala

Quality without results is pointless. Results without quality is boring.

Johan Cruyff, soccer legend

The delegates agreed to take back their findings to their respective state football federations. They also decided to set up a PVI system trial in one remote area of Australia where talent scouts rarely visited. It was an exciting time for football development. Who would have ever thought that two countries from the opposite ends of the earth, one small and one vast island continent, would come together in mutual interest?

Gunnar and Robby had one opportunity to prove the viability of the technology. If they failed, it would undoubtedly mean curtains for the project. They were under immense pressure and scrutiny to justify the benefits of the PVI system.

It was Gunnar's last day in Sydney, and the harbour city

put on a display of warmth, charm, and character. They were seated at a café, with Robby facing the Sydney Harbour Bridge and picturesque views of Darling Harbour. It was going to be difficult for Gunnar to leave this beautiful city.

So much had been achieved in the last couple of days, and the best was yet to come. A meeting was scheduled between them and the new sensation in Australian football, Harry Duwala. If you had never heard of him, it would only be a matter of time before he became a household name. There was something about Harry that stood out among all the players that had participated in the trial. It was reminiscent of Gunnar's exploits in Iceland when he had discovered talented players from the most inconspicuous of places. He described Harry in the same way as his best discoveries in Icelandic football, and he was about to explain why. However, he had been holding back something special and was ready to unleash the power of the PVI system like never before.

"Tell me, what is it about Harry that makes you so excited?" Robby asked.

"My dear friend, there is something I want to share with you first, and I want you to promise to keep it to yourself."

"You have my word. But what is it?" He leaned forward with his elbow on the table, looking directly at Gunnar. It was a poignant poise.

"When I developed the drone for the PVI system, I added a feature that will revolutionise world football talent identification." Gunnar paused for a moment. "I have been testing the new feature successfully in Iceland for the last year."

"That sounds exciting." He was drowning in anticipation.

"I added the player football values module to the assessment. I can now measure the players' attitudes with one another and the team when they perform technical manoeuvres."

"You're kidding me!" Robby was in awe.

"Yes, values in football are so important." His face exuded sincerity. "I can now measure team play, communication, respect for oneself and others, perseverance, and self-belief during gameplay."

This astonished Robby. "So how on earth can you accurately measure a player's values? Does the data reliably measure them?"

"That is a great question. All coaches and talent scouts have grappled with this issue," Gunnar said.

"I remember Johan Cruyff once said that a football player has a big social responsibility and that he is an example to many."

"That is true. A player that does not demonstrate good values in society is unlikely to make it in Icelandic football." Gunnar lifted his glass and took a sip of water. "It's in our culture and the way we bring up our children, and football is an extension of those values."

"Is that what stood out when we discovered Harry Duwala?" Robby was keen to connect the dots.

"Yes, and I didn't want to talk about football values with the delegates yesterday because it can be a controversial topic."

"I understand it wasn't the right time."

"As for your question about the reliability of data, I have done several tests and permutations for one year to get it right.' Gunnar took another sip of water. "I believe the current refinement to the values module and syncing with the drone has eliminated several false readings."

"It looks like you have done a lot of work around this, Gunnar. I am so impressed."

"But that is not all . . . ."

"You have something else in mind?"

"I want to let you in on a secret." Gunner paused. "I am developing something special, but it won't be ready for twelve months."

"What is it? I'm curious."

"I have developed a new generation sock that is built on

nanotechnology that protects the player for being injured around the leg and ankle." Gunnar had a grin on his face. "It's in development phase."

"When can I see it?"

"I will send you a sample when it's in prototype mode." Gunnar looked at Robby directly in the eye. "You need to keep it to yourself . . . you're the only one that knows."

"Yes. You have my word."

So strong was the professional relationship that they could talk for hours. However, both agreed to call it quits and prepare for their next meeting. It would be Gunnar's final task in Australia before leaving the following day for the arduous trip to Iceland.

Meeting a young, shy, and impressionable Harry Duwala was next on their agenda, and they were looking forward to sharing their findings with him, for Gunnar had a lot of experience in communicating with young players and then nurturing them through structured career pathways.

Harry wasn't a city boy with parents splashing lots of money on his football development. He had a humble background in the Australian Outback, far away from the hustle and bustle of the cosmopolitan lifestyle. He did not wear fancy branded sportswear and expensive boots. If you looked closely, his clothes were either second-hand gear or from a local Kmart store. Some of the city kids would have found him odd or out of place. Others would have made fun of him because of his looks, and it was noticeable during the previous trial sessions that the city kids didn't mix it with the boys from Alice Springs. They did not make them feel welcome at the club either. The city boys were not interested in making their visitors feel at home in Blacktown.

Harry had a unique look about him and wasn't your typical suburban kid. His indigenous background had graced him with a sculptured face and slender body. He had long, skinny athletic legs that allowed him to glide through players like a gazelle. It was like watching poetry come to life as he maintained balance and poise synonymous among champion footballers. With a low sense of gravity and creative improvisation, it made him unpredictable and challenging to read. He left players guessing, would he turn left, or right? He had terrific acceleration and stamina, which meant he worked hard chasing other players when not in possession of the ball. Harry didn't expect other players to do the work for him, and neither did he model himself on English Premier League champions. He was happy to be Harry, the desert rose, an unassuming boy from the bush. He had a great work ethic and understood the meaning of putting in the effort to achieve a result for the team.

He wasn't a dirty player, and he respected others and their abilities. Quite often, he would pat another player on the back with a smile after a great shot for a goal or a manoeuvre that impressed him. He had developed a quick passing technique and close ball control. His execution accuracy was in the high nineties and showed up on the PVI system at a high standard.

His raw talent didn't come from years of skills workshops, individual coaching, or expensive football development programs. It was pure natural ability and an innate love of expressing himself on the pitch. He had learned to play football in the schoolyard with friends and during occasional inter-school matches. Harry improvised a lot from watching football on television and replicating what he saw by kicking the ball around in his backyard. It was simple, unsophisticated, and unplanned.

His parents had never played football, so he didn't have their experience to guide him through the machinations of the sport. He was a fairy tale, a freak, one in a million. A generational player that only appeared once every fifty years. Harry might not have been discovered if not for his invitation to trial in Blacktown. He would have slipped through the system as many had done before him. How many gems like Harry remained undiscovered because they could not be found using traditional scouting methods?

Harry stepped off the minibus with a slight hop, and the liaison officer directed him towards Gunnar and Robby in the club lounge at Blacktown City FC. Harry made his way towards a quiet corner of the dining lounge where they were seated. His medium-length, black hair that covered his ears was unfashionable, but it suited him. With big brown piercing eyes and an angular face, he stood out among the crowd of players from the local area.

"Hi, I am Harry," he said in a country type slang. You could tell he wasn't from the city.

"Hi, Harry. It's very nice to meet you. I am Gunnar from Iceland, and I have many things to talk to you about." He pointed to the chair and asked Harry to sit down next to Robby.

"It's nice to meet you, Gunnar."

"And this is Robby; you may have seen him at the trials in the past week."

Robby smiled and pulled out the seat for him.

"Oh yes, I have seen him around. Hi, Robby."

"Let me explain why we are talking to you." Gunnar paused, wanting to choose his words carefully. "During your trial sessions at Blacktown, you would have seen the drone flying above you and a technician at the computer hub."

"Oh, yes! That was amazing watching all of that happening around us. The technical director explained it to us."

"Harry, the data on you was excellent, and it confirmed, based on my previous experience and analysis, that you have some special talents for football." Gunnar sipped from his glass of water and continued. "There are standards in the system based on previous trials and experimentation to identify particular talents found in successful players."

Harry looked bewildered. "What does that mean?"

"Harry, it means you're an extraordinary player, and your skills and values towards your football scored very high on our system."

"I was better than the city boys?"

"You were more than better," Gunnar said enthusiastically. "You were miles ahead of them."

"I can't believe it!"

"It's not often we see this type of talent profile in our algorithm, and when this happens, I like to talk to the player to inform them of their special talent."

"Thanks for telling me this. I feel very excited." Harry looked down momentarily, not knowing what to say next.

"Let me explain better because there are several attributes, I look for in a player that my system identifies." Gunnar pulled out his iPad and retrieved a presentation that he usually provided to players to keep things simple. "I look for your ability to play as a teammate, responsibility to your team members, respect for yourself and others, your technique, and the capacity to learn and develop."

Harry didn't know what to say. "Ah. Really . . . I didn't know that at all."

"Yes, it's about football values and how you integrate as a team member."

"My grandmother always talked about these values when I was growing up, and I understand them."

"It sounds like your grandmother was a lovely person." Gunnar crossed his arms, looking directly at Harry. "Players that have these values while growing up and practised by their parents tend to carry them onto the football pitch. I call it 'living the values.'"

"Thanks for sharing that with me," Harry said. "What happens now? Are you going to watch me for a little longer?"

"The purpose of our talk today is also to inform you that I have a spot for you on the talented players' program here in Sydney."

"I have been selected?"

"Oh yes, more than selected."

"I can't believe it!" Harry was excited, thrusting his hand in the air.

"The only issue is you need to stay in Sydney for six months, and you need to talk to your parents." Gunnar wasn't comfortable breaking the news that Harry may need to separate from his family at such a young age. "Do you have any relatives in Sydney that can help you?"

"I have an uncle, and that's it. We don't see him very often."

"In terms of living expenses, you don't need to worry. The program will obtain special funding because you are from a remote location."

"That's a great help because I don't think it's something Mum and Dad could afford."

"Yes, it is a great help. However, it's always best in my experience for the player to stay with people they know."

"I will talk to my parents tonight and see if they are OK with it."

"I am leaving for Iceland tomorrow and want to give you my email address so we can stay in contact."

"Thanks a lot, Gunnar. By the way, where is Iceland?"

Gunnar wasn't surprised by the question as he was often asked about the location of his country, and he smiled at Harry. "Let me show you a map on my iPad where Iceland is located."

The conversation continued for another half hour before Harry made his way to his last training session at

Blacktown City FC. When Gunnar left to catch his flight back to Iceland, Robby offered to walk Harry to the pitch and continue the conversation.

Robby understood he had a big task ahead of him. Trying to lure a sixteen-year-old boy from regional Australia and the security of a close community was going to be challenging. Unless he had the support of Harry's family and a way of getting him accommodated in the vast Sydney sprawl, the whole process was doomed. He wasn't going to let this fantastic talent walk away, and in the meantime, he needed to arrange another session with the PVI system.

The system required obtaining more algorithms on Harry to reinforce the previous findings. Call it re-assurance and making sure the player wasn't a one-hit-wonder. He would send the drone to a prearranged venue near Harry's hometown of Alice Springs for trails in the local area. It would involve his local football club, Alice Springs Celtic FC, and the potential to screen other players in the local area at the same time.

Robby would continue to manage the implementation of the PVI system in Australia and nurture players like Harry. He was an excellent mentor to young aspiring football players. The PVI process required multiple assessments over some time. Harry had to be analysed further with additional player identification sessions.

If the trials went according to plan, the Football Federation of Australia had agreed to purchase the PVI system and the drone under license from Gunnar's company. He would be anointed the head of talented player identification and granted full management rights to the PVI system. Robby would commence work on a scheduled plan in remote locations around Australia. It was a smart move, considering his knowledge of the system, process, and unique relationship with Gunnar.

He walked back to the pitch with Harry briskly. He was running late for their last session, and this would not impress the coach, who was a stickler for time.

"So, tell me, Harry, how do you feel when you are playing football?'

Harry had some shy tendencies about him. He didn't want to answer straight away and paused. When he responded, he tilted his head down.

"You know . . . I feel the energy going right through my body, and it feels like electricity." Harry looked directly at him. "I know where everyone is around me, and by the time I get the ball, I know what to do."

"So you know what will be your next move straight away?"

"Yeah. It's a split-second thing, and I don't know where

it comes from." Harry tightened his grip on his backpack, as it was falling to the side. "I think it's a natural thing for me."

"That's special, and in my thirty years of football, I have only had the pleasure of meeting one player that ever described that feeling to me."

"So you have heard of this before?"

"Oh, yes. It's an exceptional talent to have." He had an immense smile on his face. "I call it 'living the game.'"

"What does that mean?"

"It means you were born with exceptional talent and the ability to feel and live the game differently than other players."

Harry didn't know how to comprehend this. "I had no idea. I thought it was a normal thing."

"It's far from normal. It's extraordinary, and only elite players have this dimension to their game." He looked directly at Harry. "I guess you were born with it . . . and it's not something you can teach a player."

"Wow. I didn't expect that."

"I'll leave you here and let you get on with your training. I have all your details and will be in contact with you about the next steps of assessment next week." He pulled his business card from his wallet and handed it over to Harry. "Here, put this in your bag. I understand you're leaving back home tonight."

"Yes. Catching a flight with the boys at nine p.m. to Alice Springs."

"If you need help discussing anything with your parents about the next steps, you have my number."

"Thanks."

"Do you mind if I watch you train for the next thirty minutes? I have some time to kill now that Gunnar has left."

"Yeah, sure. Good to have you around," Harry said.

"Great."

Harry was grouped up with his friends from Alice Springs and players from various parts of Sydney: the city boys. The other group consisted of players selected from last year's trials that already had been in the development program for a year. All the players were juggling for final spaces, and the previous training day was critical for those that were hanging by a thread. Today was a serious session, and the selector had made that very clear before they were split up into teams.

The match between the two groups commenced at a frantic pace with high intensity. Unlike the previous sessions, it was every man for himself.

Harry was in fine form and playing in his usual midfield attacking role. His change of direction, close ball control, and variable pace dazzled his opponents. They could not get the ball off him as he continuously used his attacking prowess to unsettle his opponents until a crunching slide tackle ferociously challenged him.

Harry flew over his opponent on contact, landing solidly on his back, and clasping his ankle. He was in pain. In an official match, the defender would have been sent from the field of play for a reckless challenge. His colleagues assembled around him to see what assistance they could provide while others pushed and shoved the opposing players. There was a high level of dissatisfaction, and several trainers had to settle the players down to prevent the game from getting out of control. It was ugly, deliberate, and an unprofessional challenge specifically motivated to hurt him.

Harry was calm and managed to contain his emotions. He stood up, limping on his right leg, and continued to shrug it off by walking around and applying pressure to the injured area. He had a calm demeanour and did not retaliate. He didn't complain to the offending player and was determined to continue playing as he jogged back into position.

The game continued, and so did the shenanigans by the other team—they were hell-bent on getting Harry and making sure he had no further part to play. The game was played at a frantic pace, and you would have thought that it was a cup final rather than a training session.

There was an excellent long pass to Harry on the right-wing as the team switched the field of play to take full advantage of a breakaway move. He gathered the ball, sweetly passing not one but three defenders with tantalising ball control as he outwitted each of them with all sorts of trickery. He was a fantastic player to watch. As he made his final run towards the goal, he was brought down again by a second crunching slide tackle. This time it was a different player with the same motive. It was a deliberate tackle to his left ankle with no intent to play the ball.

Robby could not believe what he was witnessing. He wanted to intervene and remove Harry from the game for his safety. He was tempted to run on the pitch to help but realised it would have been inappropriate to interfere in a training session, so he reluctantly remained steadfast.

Scuffles broke out again between the two teams, and the game degenerated into pushing, shoving, and verbal altercations. Harry lifted himself from the ground, dusted the grass from his uniform and limped his way to the bench. He did not need assistance to get off the field and could walk unattended, and that was a good sign that he had avoided serious injury.

As for the remaining part of the game, the football

trainer called the players in and had a stern word with all of them, mainly the offending player that had laid the horrible tackle on him. Judging by the conversation between the trainer and the offending player, he was unlikely to be selected. Players that engaged in behaviour to deliberately hurt their opponent showed a lack of respect to others, and this didn't go down well with the football selectors.

Harry was limping from a swollen ankle. Robby was well aware that a severe ankle injury could take four to six weeks to heal. That wasn't going to help his discussion with Harry's parents. The last thing he wanted was to be talking to his parents about a move to Sydney with an injury cloud hanging over things. Experience told him it was not a good time. His parents would ask questions about his injury and how it came about. It could turn against him and end his playing career. In one moment of madness, a crunching and deliberate tackle may have changed the pendulum on his playing future.

6 | Chasing Celtic FC

The most pleasure any manager can get is seeing every day boys joining the club as youngsters and growing into men and giving themselves a better social standing than they could ever have dreamed of previously.

Jock Stein, Football Manager Celtic FC

As the red desert sun rose above the MacDonnell Ranges and the red earth landscape, a large gathering was taking place at Alice Springs Celtic FC. There was a buzz around the club, and an air of enthusiasm as the locals embraced the trial. They had come from all over the Alice and its surrounding communities to participate. Once, it would have been unheard of that a remote Australian town would host such an event.

Robby waited for everyone to settle in the clubroom as people gathered patiently at the entrance. It was standing room only as participants squeezed in together.

"Dear family and friends, I am privileged today to welcome you to your home club and host of the trials . . . it's a fantastic turnout. I am so happy to see so many people. Our trials would not have been possible without the coordination and efforts of your club's management team. I want to thank them for their support.

"Things will get underway soon, and I ask all trialists to make their way to the computer hub outside this room and register their armbands. Due to the unexpectedly high number of trialists, armbands will be refitted after each trial session. There will be at least five trial sessions during the day to ensure everyone is involved.

"The data obtained from the trial is private and will only be shared with your coaching director to assess you individually. You will be advised about further assessments if you meet the standards. It's not a one-off process and will involve new trials for those that are selected.

"Next to me is Harry Duwala. He attended the Sydney trials in Blacktown as part of your indigenous exchange program. He was identified from a very competitive group of players. Nobody knew who he was until the PVI system identified him, and it serves as an example of what is achievable."

There was a round of applause directed to Harry and his achievements. "Good on ya, Harry!" one of the parents said. He had become an example of what was possible, and local players embraced him as a shining light in the Alice.

Robby concluded the presentation and turned towards

Harry with a bright smile. "Thanks for your help. I appreciate it so much."

"I'm happy to help the boys from around here," he said while fiddling with his ponytail. "There are so many good players here wanting to impress."

"If we can find one more player like you, I will be over the moon!"

Harry blushed while tucking both hands into his pockets. He wasn't used to all this attention, particularly from scouts like Robby. "Everyone in town and the surrounding communities have been talking about the trials."

"I didn't realise we would have such an interest."

"Yes, it's been a big thing." Harry paused to gather his breath and to ask an important question. It had been bothering him for a while. "There is one thing I wanted to ask you."

"Yes?"

"My parents want to meet you today after the trials."

"It would be great to meet them, and I expected it anyway."

"Yes, but a warning: they don't like the idea of me moving to Sydney." Harry was uncomfortable with the conversation and struggled to find the right words. "They are saying I'm too young."

"How do you feel about that?"

Harry's face changed from cheerfulness to sadness as his glowing smile withered away. "It's what I want to do more than anything else in the world."

"It's not an easy position to be in, and I can understand their concerns. Didn't you have an uncle in Sydney that could help you with your stay?" Robby asked.

"Yes, and I spoke to my parents about it."

"And?"

"Made no difference."

"Did you tell them the academy would be paying your expenses and that our community grant will fund your stay in Sydney?"

"Yes, but it's not just about the money." He looked directly at Robby. It was turning out to be a difficult discussion for both of them.

"I'll tell you what: let's not pre-empt the discussion with your parents."

"What do you mean?"

"If they raise it with me, I will reassure them that I will be your mentor and look out for you the best way I can."

"Can you do that?"

"It's the least I can do. I don't want to see your talent wasted, but at the same time, I need to give your parents the confidence you will be looked after." Robby had a lot of experience nurturing young players and had encountered similar situations before. "Did I ever tell you the story of the Australian football legend that played for Liverpool during the eighties, Craig Johnston?"

"No, I have never heard of him."

"It was before your time, but it's something I would like to share with you."

"Sure. I always enjoy your stories about champions."

"Craig Johnston took up football in Newcastle, and at the age of fourteen, he wrote to four English clubs seeking a trial. Among those was Manchester United and Chelsea." He sipped on some water, as his mouth was becoming dry from all the talking. "The Middlesbrough manager, Jack Charlton, replied, and he travelled to England."

"Really!"

"Yes, and as a fifteen-year-old, Johnston stayed at Middlesbrough for six months."

"He was my age."

"That's right. However, not everything went according to plan at the beginning, and it was tough for him."

"Oh? Tell me more." Harry was getting curious.

"The word is that Jack Charlton told Craig Johnston he was the worst player he'd ever seen." He paused to recall the rest of the story. "To prove to his club manager he was worth considering; he practised for many hours a day to get better until Jack Charlton was replaced as Middlesbrough manager by John Neal."

"So he wasn't any good?"

"Oh no . . . he was good. It was how he proved himself that is inspiring."

"Oh!"

"When John Neal came to Middlesbrough as the new manager, he saw Craig training in the car park by himself."

"What sort of training did he do?"

"He kicked the ball on the wall and made targets to refine his kicking ability for hours on end."

"I guess a lot of players would have given up and gone home." Harry was becoming more intrigued by the story.

"John Neal asked some of the apprentices who he was, and they said, 'He's here from half-past six in the morning, and he's still here when we leave.'"

"What happened after that?"

"John Neal was impressed by his determination, and the rest is history."

"So, he got his chance?" Harry asked.

"Yes, he went on to play sixty-four matches for Middlesbrough and 190 matches for Liverpool, one FA Cup, and five league titles."

"That is so impressive!" Harry could relate to the story and was enthused.

"I thought you would like the story. My point is that playing football and having the inspiration to be the best requires sacrifice, and it does not come easy."

"Maybe you can share that story with my parents?"

"Sure. I have nothing to lose."

Harry smiled, realising he had been handed a lifeline. Robby was a great motivator, and young footballers liked him for his encouragement.

Since that day in Blacktown six months ago, a lot had happened in a short time frame, and many things had fallen into place. The PVI system and the equipment arrived from Iceland intact, and with the help of Magnus, the technical expert, they managed to get everything synchronised and working correctly. The drone had flown several test flights on the outskirts of Sydney and was communicating player algorithms back to the hub. The Mark II model of the drone had a longer reach and could stay in the air for extended periods. That meant access to more remote places.

Robby learned a new skill and became a qualified drone pilot, which was a requirement to operate the flying machines. He immersed himself in his newfound passion. It was challenging to get the joystick from Robby during practice flights; such was the enjoyment and thrill to pilot the machine. He also had to complete training in navigation so that he could input the coordinates into the drone.

The trial session today had been arranged in Alice Springs at a local football club with a rich history in the local area. Robby reflected on the invitation brochure that Alice Springs Celtic FC had sent to him.

Alice Springs Celtic is an Australian football club based in the city of Alice Springs, and is a member of the Football Federation Northern Territory. It has seen great success in recent years, becoming premiers in 2015 and champions in 2016.

Scottish immigrant Billy Reilly, who knew Celtic FC player and manager Jock Stein founded the club in 1979.

The team consisted of both Alice Springs locals and also Irish and Scottish players who were living in Alice Springs. It has the same green-and-white stripes as the Scottish premier league club Celtic.

The club's home ground is nestled between the East and West MacDonnell Ranges.

Alice Springs is located in central Australia in a remote location and often called 'the Alice' or only 'Alice.' It is called 'Mparntwe' by the Arrernte people, who have lived around Alice Springs for more than 50,000 years. The indigenous people have a rich cultural history and tradition.

Harry and his family were descendants of the Arrernte, and he was very proud of his heritage. However, they lived a typical western lifestyle in the Alice and had regular jobs in the community.

The club had welcomed Robby with open arms and a level of enthusiasm that was unexpected. Nobody ever sent scouts to the local area. It was considered Outback Australia and too remote for any significant club to invest resources in scouting their youth for talent. News that a fantastic find and interest in Harry had emerged. It was the talk of the club and the local community.

It was still not decided whether his family would allow Harry to move to Sydney to foster his ambitions, and a lot of convincing was yet required. Harry's parents made their way to Alice Springs Celtic FC to speak to Robby. As discussions go, the future of Harry's playing career was in their hands. As a minor, he needed their permission to participate in the talent development program. In the worst-case scenario, Harry would need to wait until eighteen years of age to make his own decision. However, two years was a long time in player development. Without a structured program to help him develop and fulfil his potential, Harry's career could take a turn in the wrong direction. So much was hanging in the balance, and Robby was acutely aware of the circumstances.

Harry was feeling apprehensive about the meeting in front of the clubrooms at Alice Springs Celtic FC. "Robby, please meet my mum and dad, Margaret and George."

Robby stood up. He was a towering figure. He put his right hand forward to greet both parents. He gently shook their hands. "Harry has mentioned a lot about your family, and I am pleased to meet you after all this time."

Margaret looked up at him. "Oh yes, and he doesn't stop talking about you too." George stood one step behind her, smiling and nodding.

"I hope he has said nothing but good things?"

"Of course, and I have never seen Harry so confident and full of belief in himself." She pointed to a spare table under the shade cloth next to the clubroom. "Should we take a seat over there? I wouldn't mind a cold drink!"

"Sounds like a great idea, and a cold drink in this heat will be perfect!"

They all sat down together as the conversation continued. However, Robby was aware the tough questions would come, and he was prepared to respond to all their concerns.

"So, I want to speak to you about Harry moving to Sydney."

"Sure, Margaret. I can explain the proposal to you." He took a deep breath and had to think quickly. "I understand how difficult this is for your family. I have had similar situations with young players throughout my career."

"Oh yes, it's not easy for a fifteen-year-old boy leaving home." She sounded croaky. "We are a close family, and he helps George fixing things around the garage, you know."

"Yeah, he mentioned how George has a repair business, and he likes dismantling things and helping out."

"Well, I think he also told you we have a relative in Sydney. It's my brother Harold, and I have spoken to him already about the possibility of Harry staying with him."

"What did he say?"

"We are very close. He grew up around here before leaving for Sydney for work."

"I see . . ."

"He will do everything that is required to care for Harry." She was being positive about the whole move but was still reluctant as any mother would be. "If it wasn't for Harold, I don't think it would be possible for Harry to move to Sydney."

"I understand because I'm also a parent, and I know what this means to you."

"When I see the light in Harry's eyes and the passion he feels about the game, how can we stop him from achieving his dreams?"

"I also see that in him all the time." Robby felt the conversation was going somewhere.

"I don't want to be the one blamed for not giving him this chance."

"I know how that feels."

"He can stay in the Alice and work in his father's garage as most boys do around here, or he can have a shot at becoming someone." Margaret's voice was breaking up, and he could see a tiny teardrop in her eye. It was an emotional time for her.

"Can I tell you the story of Charles Perkins?" He paused for a few moments. "He was a local and went on to become a great football player and advocate for indigenous people."

"Oh, we all know about Charles around here, and he did so much for our community," Margaret said.

"He did it the tough way in the early years with no support from anyone. He moved to Adelaide as a talented footballer before moving to England to try his luck all on his own."

"I didn't know he played overseas. It's tough for local indigenous boys to get discovered in the Outback."

"Not that I would like him to go through the same struggle, and I think we have progressed a lot since then. I was fortunate to be able to assess Harry in Sydney and identify his talents during trials."

"Harry mentioned that machine . . . what do you call it? Sounds very futuristic, you know."

"Yes, we call it the drone." Robby smiled.

"In most cases, Harry would have returned to the Alice with no further assessment or opportunity. Whatever you have developed in finding new talent is amazing, and we can see the buzz it's creating here with the locals," she said.

"Yes, and unlike the struggles of Charles Perkins, we have designed a program for Harry. He will be well looked after as we focus on developing his amazing talent!"

"You think he will be good enough to make it?' She paused. "I mean, for his future?"

"He's more than good. He's a revelation, and I can't remember the last time I ever saw anyone so talented."

"Really?"

"His temperament, attitude, and respect for others play an important part in his selection, apart from his amazing technical skills." Robby was warming to the idea he may have Margaret over the line.

"We always brought up Harry making sure he respects people around him and his community."

"I can see you and George have done an amazing job in the way you have brought him up."

Robby sipped on his iced tea, as he was finding the heat suffocating. There was sweat on his receding hairline, for it was apparent he wasn't acclimatised to the Alice's heat. He looked behind him and could see the technician waving.

"I think I'm wanted. Need to launch the drone."

"You can fly that thing?" Margaret was surprised.

"You wouldn't believe I had to get a flying license for it! But don't worry: I can't fly planes!"

They all giggled at his sarcastic humour. Robby was a charismatic man, and people from all walks of life felt comfortable with him. He thanked Margaret and George for meeting with him and walked over to the drone.

There was the hustle and bustle of people near him as he took control of the joystick. A crowd that had been assembling to get a glimpse of the new technology surrounded him. You would have thought the large gathering had come to watch the air show instead of a football trial.

Better get this thing off the ground, he thought.

Gunnar had sent a club pennant from Keflavík FC as an exchange gift for Alice Springs Celtic FC. It would be the beginnings of a friendship between the two clubs from the opposite ends of the earth. It comprised the blue-and-red colours of the team with the capital letter *K* in the middle. It was a gesture of respect, and he was looking forward to presenting it to the club president. Robby placed the banner on the drone so everyone could see it in the meantime.

The drone used for the trial at Alice Springs Celtic FC was the upgraded Mark II model. Several enhancements had been made to the programming and most notably the player movement algorithms. This upgrade provided a live stream for every participant to the computer hub in real-time. The player movement algorithms measured key aspects of intelligence, ability, and decision-making. As many of these decisions where split-second actions occurring multiple times in a sequence of play, it was impossible for the human eye to record this data continuously.

It was a giant leap forward for assessing players' abilities. It provided the speed of information that no human eye could match. The upgraded model took a lot of unconscious bias, influence, and subjectivity out of the assessment process.

Robby managed to get the drone in the air as it seamlessly swerved around into position. It was an imposing device for those that had never witnessed it before. Its electric engines manoeuvred above the football pitch and then remained stationary with an uncanny level of precision. Everyone was enthralled, and the participants pointed upwards in awe of this invention. You could blink once, twice, three times, and the drone didn't move. Such was the technology used to stabilise it. Robby had a grin on his face and a joyful expression as he manoeuvred the drone.

The technician operating the central hub tested the data from an armband fitted on a trialist who casually walked around the field, kicking the ball to a colleague.

Data was streaming in, and the test phase was successfully producing the information required to assess players. Everything was going according to plan and Robby was keen to get started.

All eyes around the luscious green pitch were on the drone as players eagerly awaited to be grouped into teams. At least eighty trialists were participating throughout the day.

Robby got the all-clear from the technician at the hub, and he successfully landed the drone. He launched the drone for the second time and navigated it above the playing field with the same level of precision. An electric buzzing sound was heard hovering above the centre circle.

The drone hovered in perfect steadiness, ready to start measuring the players' attributes and receiving information from the smart armbands.

The trial matches had started, and players rotated every twenty minutes to give every participant a chance to show their stuff. Even if you were not the best football player on the pitch, the PVI system ensured everyone was treated fairly and provided an opportunity to showcase their talent.

Robby started to feel an unusual vibration while controlling the movements of the drone with the joystick.

"I'm having difficulty controlling the drone. It's not responding to my joystick."

"Let me check that for you." The computer hub technician ran a quick series of tests.

"Still nothing . . ."

"I'm getting a jamming signal, and I don't know where it's coming from."

"Should you take control yourself and put it into override mode?" Robby asked.

"The override mode is not working. Let me keep trying."

Robby firmly held on to the joystick and made jagged movements. "I can't control the damn thing. It's not responding."

The technician was frantically attempting to wrestle control of the drone. "We have switched to override mode, and it's not connecting! Something is jamming our signal."

"What about the people below? We can't allow it to crash!"

The drone was hovering about the sports field, shaking and looking unstable. If they didn't manage to get control quickly, it could spell disaster.

Robby noticed a Chinese man in the distance, standing with an iPad next to a bright-green car. He looked suspiciously towards him and the drone.

I'm sensing some foul play, he thought.

"A Chinese man is standing next to a bright-green vehicle 100 metres north of you. He's holding an iPad," Robby said.

"Near the car park entrance, you mean?"

"Yes."

"Let me see what he's up to." The technician scrambled towards the Chinese man.

As he got closer to the suspect, the Chinese man saw him and became anxious. In an attempt to flee, he dropped the iPad, then picked it up. The screen was damaged. He threw the iPad into the driver's seat and fled immediately, tyres screeching as the vehicle sped out of the car park. A trail of red dust filled the air as the car swivelled left to right while almost losing control. By the time the technician made it to the car park, the Chinese man was well on his way, and there was no possibility of catching him.

"I have control back again. Everything is fine." Robby was sweating heavily from the ordeal.

"He left very quickly when he noticed me coming, but I found something," the technician said.

"What do you have?"

"It's a card, and they dropped it in a hurry. It says, 'Mission: Ninjutsu.'"

"I wonder if that means something? Leave it with me. I might raise it with Gunnar and see if there is a link with Mission Ninjutsu. He may know something about it," Robby said.

Robby decided to take a break after the near-flight disaster with the drone. He reviewed his slide presentation to the club's management team to take his mind off things.

A key objective of the trial was to educate the management team of the hosting football club on the benefits of the PVI system. The presentation for Alice Springs Celtic was to be held in the club lounge, and it provided an opportunity for the local club management team to ask questions.

At the end of his slide presentation, Robby felt compelled to finish off with a personal summary. It was unscripted and straight from the heart. No notes, no slides, nothing. He just wanted to be himself and recognise Gunnar's achievements. He stood up and spoke passionately. He felt comfortable that he could express his point of view.

"There is nothing like it in the world, and what Gunnar Grimsson has developed is remarkable. If you were a talent scout, assessor, or coach, all you can do is fall in love with this system and succumb to its prowess. It is the holy grail of world football domination. The Icelandic team has proved it with their unsurpassable performances on the international stage and talented player development. All because of one man and his quest to bring fairness back to the game.

"Gunnar had the vision to return the game to its original roots where social status and money had no bearing on your ability to play the game, it's a level playing field, and everyone has the opportunity to exploit their talents.

"The purpose of the PVI system is to find those beautiful players like Harry Duwala that were anonymous to the current scouting system. To find the desert rose where it was thought to be unobtainable. That is what drove Gunnar to develop the Player Virtual Identification system. It's what inspired me to travel to Iceland in search of football's holy grail.

"The world of football talent development has changed, and those countries that adopt this new philosophy will go on to dominate world football at all levels."

Robby concluded his presentation and took a seat. The management team acknowledged him with a round of applause.

No one had ever bothered to arrange trial sessions in the remote Outback town, and scouts had just become a word rather than a reality. They had never bothered to visit. Times had changed, and all aspiring players could trial and measure their potential in a controlled environment. Robby's sincere conclusion hit a chord with the management team at Alice Springs Celtic FC. One by one, they stood up and hugged him, patting him on the back.

The club secretary approached the front of the room and stood next to Robby.

"That was wonderful, Robby. It was the best presentation we have ever had at the club. We thank you for coming all this way to spend the day with us and educate the team on the future of football development." The club secretary handed him a small gift in appreciation. It was framed print of a desert rose with the Alice Springs Celtic FC inscription engraved at the bottom.

"Oh, I wasn't expecting this. Thanks so much." Robby was chuffed.

7 | The Nano Fit-out

Soccer, to me, is one way of breaking down the barriers between national, racial, and language difficulty.

Charles Perkins, Australia's first prolific indigenous football player

The doorbell rang, and he had not changed the chime since Christmas. "Jingle bells, jingle bells . . ." It was a cold winter morning, and he wasn't in the mood to step outside into the howling rain.

Nevertheless, he gathered the strength to put on his robe and quickly open the door. There it was, a parcel from overseas on his doorstep. It had the Icelandic post service stamp, *Íslandspóstur*, embedded in the packaging. He smiled, realising it could only have come from Gunnar.

It was a medium-sized box that could fit a shirt. Robby swiftly opened the package, ripping it on all sides. To his surprise, there was a pair of yellow football socks in a plastic sleeve with a note from Gunnar. He was keen to read the message and opened the note first.

I wonder what's in the message? he thought.

Gunnar had promised he would send Robby a surprise when he returned to Iceland twelve months ago. It was a carefully kept secret, and an aura of mystery surrounded it.

Dear Robby,

As I mentioned before leaving Sydney, here is the surprise I promised you. It's been one year in the making, and I am sure you will find it a unique product. Nothing like it exists in the world. I have recently received approval by the world football governing body FIFA as suitable plating equipment.

Icelandic national teams at all levels will use it this year. Its manufactured from a new type of nanotechnology fibre, and it flexes on impact to form a protective barrier for players.

No more shin guards required as this material has twice the protection and better freedom of movement. Players have been amazed at how light it feels and even more impressed by its protective strength.

We have significantly reduced injuries to the lower part of the leg in early trials and increased playing longevity. Put them on, and get someone to kick you! Try to rip them with a knife . . . I dare you!

Let me know your thoughts, and please keep it to yourself for now, as we don't have an international patent. Until such time, we won't be releasing it outside of Iceland.

Your good friend always, Gunnar Grimsson

PS: How is our young protégé, Harry Duwala?

That was Gunnar's style, always years ahead of anyone else. A stalwart in finding solutions to problems that no one considered. Robby knew that when it arrived, it would be special.

He was recapping his last conversation with Gunnar when they had dined in Sydney. He had discussed his new project to revolutionise player equipment. He wasn't trying to start a new brand of clothing company but a new technology-focused on player protection. He recalled a meaningful conversation about how current equipment didn't offer sufficient protection against injuries.

There was a list of players Gunnar had sent to his email whose careers had ended prematurely due to preventable injuries. These players were household names in world football. Their injuries had denied them a long-term career and robbed the public of their talents. Driven by curiosity, Robby opened his laptop to find the email Gunnar had sent him.

I never really paid much attention to this until now, he thought.

The list caught his attention, and he was unaware such talented players had their amazing carers robbed by injury. He was a Manchester City fan, and players like Alf-Inge Håland and Colin Bell were very familiar to him during his childhood years. They were household names back then. He also remembered great talents like Brian Clough at Sunderland and Pierluigi Casiraghi, the Italian who had played at Chelsea. Gunnar's new technology may not have saved their careers, but what if they could have played longer?

He had a plan. He would contact Harry and ask him to meet before his next training session.

Maybe I will get Harry to try them on for me and give me some feedback, he thought. *I can trust him to keep it to himself.*

He was aware of the benefits new playing equipment would provide teams competing on the world stage. Teams that sustained fewer injuries and critical players sidelined during tournaments could outperform their opponents.

What if the injuries were less severe and recovery was quicker, and they could make a comeback sooner than expected? Teams that had this technology could dominate world football by putting the best team on the park all of the time.

He was partway through his five-kilometre walk along the northern shoreline of Sydney. He had walked the same path for the last five years. Weight management always had been a problem, as he loved to eat and regularly dine out. He had culinary tastes from all over the world and was open-minded about cuisines. His long walks kept him reasonably fit for a man of his maturing years. Considering he was fifty, he was in good shape and didn't suffer from common medical concerns such as diabetes or high cholesterol.

Robby felt his phone vibrate in his pocket and briskly removed it. He checked the screen.

Gunnar is trying to call me, he thought. *Must be about the socks.*

"Hello, my good friend," he said enthusiastically. "I think I know why you are calling me."

"Ha, ha! Checking if you received my big surprise."

"Oh yes, the surprise was a big one even though the parcel was small!"

"So, you liked the socks?"

"Like is an understatement. I never imagined you could make socks like that from nanotechnology."

Gunnar responded with a sigh. "Have you have tried it out already?"

"Only you could come up with something like that. How on earth could you invent a product that prevents injury by transforming into a protective barrier on impact?"

"So, you have tested it?"

"Not yet."

"I'm sure you will like it?" Gunnar said.

"It sounds revolutionary!"

"I knew you would like my surprise." Gunnar was excited. "We are starting to use the socks for our national teams to reduce injury, and so far, the stats are showing a seventy-five percent reduction in shin and ankle injuries."

"Those are amazing numbers, and I believe it." He wanted to know more. "Are you going to continue working on other player equipment?"

"I had a feeling you would ask me that." Gunnar was ready. He understood Robby and his thirst to know everything in detail.

"Well?"

"Socks are the beginning, and eventually, I will be looking at shorts and shirts with the same technology," he said.

"Why doesn't that surprise me?" Robby sat down on a park bench and welcomed the short rest.

"And one thing . . ."

"Yes."

"Please keep this technology to yourself for now. We don't want it to get into the hands of our competition."

"I completely understand this is going to give the Icelandic team an edge in player management. You have World Cup qualifiers coming up soon." Robby wiped the sweat from his forehead with the sleeve of his tracksuit jacket.

"That's right, and I'm sure during our first qualifier everyone will be asking why the Icelandic team is wearing no shin guard protection."

"Is that when you will communicate it to the football public?" Robby asked.

"Yes, I think I will have no choice, as many commentators will be asking questions. Our public relations person has got that in hand."

"I look forward to it."

"Hey, Robby, got to go now, but I am thrilled you got to see the socks and try them out."

"Yes. When you say surprise, you mean it!"

"I miss our conversations. Take care and say hello to Harry for me. I'm happy he's progressing well."

"Yes, he's doing very well. I will pass on your regards to him."

He had enjoyed his conversation with Gunnar, although it was short. He was frustrated because there was more he had wanted to ask him. Gunnar never did anything half-hearted, and the socks were just the beginning.

He recalled a conversation he had had with Gunnar when he was in Sydney about his despair when players were injured and how little was done to prevent it from happening. The focus had been on treatment, but little had changed in preventing players from sustaining injuries in the first place. He had not seriously latched on to the conversation at the time and had thought Gunnar was venting.

Robby met with Harry the next day at the same training venue every Wednesday. It was their regular catch-up day and an opportunity to check on how he was doing. Robby had promised Harry's parents he would take care of Harry, and he wasn't going to let them down.

"Harry, come over here. I want you to kick me in the shin."

"Say that again?"

"Yes, you heard me right. Kick me here."

"Are you sure about this? What if I injure you?"

"It's ok. Do it. Nothing to worry. I promise."

Harry reluctantly pulled his leg back and kicked him, but in a measured way.

Robby stood motionless and with a cheeky grin. "Is that the best you can do?"

"How come you didn't feel anything?"

"Ha, ha. That was nothing. Kick me harder!"

"OK, if that's what you want." Harry pulled back his leg even farther to simulate a stronger tackle.

Robby laughed and said, "I didn't feel a thing. Do you think you try a little harder?"

"Robby, what on earth is underneath your sock? I can't see any padding that may be cushioning it. Is this some trick?"

"It's a new sock Gunnar sent me. I'm testing it out."

"What? I can't believe it!"

"I promised Gunnar we would keep it to ourselves until it's officially launched."

"Sure, but do you mind if I take the sock with me to training and test them further?"

Robby paused. "Some further testing would be helpful."

"I promise to be discreet. I can wear it underneath my usual socks so nobody can see them," Harry said.

"Maybe we can catch up in a couple of days, and you can tell me what you think of the sock after training?"

"I think that is a plan."

8 | FOOTBALL MISSION: NINJUTSU

The work of a team should always embrace a great player, but the great player must always work.

Sir Alex Ferguson, Football Manager Manchester United

A Chinese man wearing a grey cap and a long dark-blue jacket briskly walked towards Robby. He didn't look like your typical talent scout.

"Good morning, sir," he said with a distinctive English accent. "That was a great match. The Australian team has improved a lot during the past two years, and I am impressed."

"Oh yeah, it's the first time the team has made the semi-finals of an international tournament for twenty years." He smiled and was excited about the outcome. "China also has improved, and it was great to see them progress this far in the tournament." Robby paused and was not sure what to say next.

He had finished watching the quarter-final of the under 20 football World Cup at the Shanghai Stadium. China was the host of the tournament, with matches organised in ten major cities. China bowed out of the competition in front of a packed and raucous crowd after losing to a solitary goal against the Australians.

"My name is Wang Shu," he said. "I am pleased to meet you."

"I'm Robby Denehy. Likewise, I am pleased to meet you." He paused for a moment. "You speak English with an English accent."

"Ha, ha. I get that a lot. My family grew up in Hong Kong, and I studied at the international school. That's where I learned my English."

"That explains it. What do you do for a living?" He waited patiently for a response. "Are you a journalist?"

"Oh no, far from it," Wang said with a grin. "I'm a football scout for the Chinese Football Federation and involved in player talent identification."

"Well, so am I. We have similar roles." He was pleased to meet a likeminded individual. "I have never seen you before at major tournaments . . . are you new to scouting?"

"I don't get to travel much because of family reasons. It can be a very consuming job." Wang changed the subject. "You have an outstanding player on your team, and everyone is impressed with him. He's getting lots of interest."

"You mean Harry Duwala?"

"Yes, Harry. He was a handful for our defenders. Where did you find such amazing talent?"

Robby tried to avoid the question. "Did you like his goal?"

"It was world-class!" Wang said with a grin. "You know, even though we lost the game, the Chinese spectators appreciated his playing ability and the amazing goal he scored."

He welcomed Wang's comments. "That's what I admire about football. It crosses all boundaries, and everyone admires a quality player, no matter where they come from."

"Oh yes," Wang agreed. "That is the beauty of football." He took a seat next to him. "I have a proposition for you."

"Oh, do you? What is it?"

"Well, we have been studying Harry for some time, and our biggest club in China is interested in him," Wang said.

It came out of left field. "I'm not his agent."

"Yes, we know that. However, you're well connected with Harry, and I understand he listens to you." Wang pulled out his business card. "We can offer him a contract with the same sort of money he would get in Europe. On top of that, we guarantee him playing time."

"So, you are making Harry an offer?"

"Yes, most definitely." Wang placed his card on Robby's notepad. "Think about it and give me a call. I will be here until the end of the tournament, and it looks like you will be staying for the semi-final match in a couple of days."

"Yes, I will be. I need to speak to Harry about your offer but not until after the tournament. I don't want to distract him now."

"I understand entirely," Wang said. "Oh, and by the way: I've heard about this new technology you have been using to scout players."

"Oh yes . . . what have you heard?"

"It has been successful for your football federation," Wang said, probing for information. "Maybe that's how you found Harry?"

"You seem to know much about it."

"Yes, we have been trying to get in contact with the inventor in Iceland, Gunnar Grimsson." Wang stood up, ready to leave. "He doesn't return our calls . . . but we understand you know him very well."

"We have become good friends over time and I know he is very busy."

"Perhaps after we get Harry a professional contract in China, we could work together and develop this technology in China?" Wang was persistent and trying hard to entice him.

Robby didn't like where the conversation was going, but he had enough experience in professional football not to be surprised. "We have a license agreement with the Icelandic Football Federation, and it has a confidentiality clause. I don't think it's something I could discuss with you at this time."

"Sure. I appreciate that you have a licensing obligation," Wang said.

Robby wasn't sure what to say, so he stood silently.

"All I am asking is that you put in a good word to Gunnar to meet with us," Wang said with a poignant grin.

"You're interested in the Player Virtual Identification system?"

"Yes, and the drone technology too." He looked directly into Robby's eyes. "We will pay you handsomely as an intermediary."

"Thank you, Wang. It's not something I can commit to at the moment."

"Think about it. We can talk again soon." Wang shook his hand. "It's been a pleasure to meet a like-minded scout in world football." He paused for a moment. "Oh, and good luck with the semi-final match. I wish your team every success." He waved to Robby as he was leaving and said, "I'm sure your team will do well and progress to the next stage."

Robby was doubtful about the conversation that had just taken place. Even though Wang Shu appeared to be a gentleman, had he attempted to bribe him? Was the offer for a high-paying professional career for Harry a trade-off for the PVI system? It wasn't the first time the Chinese had made efforts to secure the technology. Unsure what to do next, he thought about discussing it with Gunnar.

Robby was confident that an offer from a reputable English Premier League club wasn't far away. Many scouts from Europe were at the match watching Harry's performance. They would leave the game feeling upbeat about his potential on the world stage. It had been a good tournament for Harry; he was in the lead to win the Golden Boot with eight goals in the competition. He was turning heads and attracting the attention of big-name clubs. Harry was scheduled to compete in the semi-final playoff for the under 20 World Cup tournament in Shanghai Stadium the next day.

Robby was to meet Gunnar for dinner at the five-star Ritz-Carlton in Shanghai that evening. He was travelling with the Icelandic under 20 representative team that had progressed to the semi-final stage. It had been a while since they had met in person, and he was looking forward to discussing the progress of the Player Virtual Identification system.

Late that evening, Robby waited at the entrance of the hotel lobby and noticed Gunnar making his way towards him. He waved at him to get his attention.

"Hello, my good Aussie friend," Gunnar said.

They hugged and patted each other on the back.

"So, how have you been?" Gunnar asked.

"I am terrific, Gunnar, and you have not changed a bit."

They took a seat at the main bar of the Ritz-Carlton. "I don't think they sell Icelandic Viking beer . . . and you may need to settle on a good Aussie pale."

"Nothing wrong with that," Gunnar said. "How about Crown Lager?" He had become acquainted with the Australian ale since his visit to Sydney.

"Sounds good to me!" He looked towards the bar attendant and raised his hand. "Two Crown Lagers, please."

"The Australians have been doing well in the tournament, and Harry is setting the whole place alight. How about that? Leading goal scorer and odds on for the Golden Boot." Gunnar was excited and would always stake his claim about finding Harry.

"I am so proud of him, and if it weren't for the PVI system, nobody would have known about his amazing talents."

"His parents are also here to watch him play, and they have never set foot on a plane before." Robby swallowed his beer like a drunken sailor. "Ah . . . now, that's a beer!" he said.

"Ha, ha. You always liked your beer."

"I need to ask you something sensitive."

"What is it?"

"Something unusual happened today at the stadium. A Chinese talent scout approached me about Harry, and then the discussion took on a different twist."

"Well, what about?"

"It turned out being a discussion about the PVI system."

"Really?" Gunnar was intrigued. "Tell me more."

"Can you shed any light on who they maybe?" Robby looked at him inquisitively. He wanted the inside scoop.

"I think I may have some answers for you." Gunnar put down his glass. "Have you heard of ninjutsu?"

"Some form of martial art, isn't it?"

"The theory is the same. Ninjutsu is the strategy and tactics of unconventional warfare, guerrilla warfare, and espionage purportedly practised by the ninja."

"What's that got to do with football?" Robby asked.

"What I'm about to tell you is very confidential."

"I promise you; my lips are sealed." He waited impatiently for Gunnar to reveal his information.

"There is a group of Chinese operatives that are after my technology; in fact, they are so desperate for it they have offered me a handsome sum of money." Gunnar paused and sipped on his beer. "But I told them I wasn't happy with their philosophy, and I declined to sell it to them. It's the same operatives you encountered in Iceland during the conference, and they are all part of the same group."

"What was it about their philosophy you didn't like?"

"They had no intention of using the PVI system to develop young talent and discover new players. They wanted to use it to spy on other countries."

"Like a spy drone? I am starting to connect the dots now." Robby nodded his head in agreement.

"Our security police found out about this coercive group from the information they received from our counterparts on the mainland. We have learned the Chinese Football Federation is paying their operatives to get the technology. It's called 'the Ninjutsu mission,'" Gunnar said.

"They wanted me to broker a meeting with you but I politely avoided the request. I had a feeling it was more than just a meeting they were after…didn't feel right."

"My advice is to stay away from them. This group will beg, steal, and do anything to get a hand on my drone and the programming system with all the player algorithms."

"Oh, I see. I'm glad I asked you." Robby sculled the rest of his beer and didn't leave a drop. "Another one?" he offered. He was aware of Gunnar's fondness for Australian beer.

"How can I say no to you?" They both smiled and ordered another round.

As the evening wore on, they continued drinking. Gunnar was able to communicate with the bartender in Chinese and eventually find the Viking beer from Iceland. He could always find a way to deliver his message. As usually happens after several glasses of excellent ale, the truth came out, and Gunnar was no different. He was having a good time and became less guarded. It was enough for him to explain the other parts of the story regarding the Chinese operatives that he had kept to himself due to security reasons from Icelandic intelligence.

He disclosed that the Chinese operative detained in Reykjavík had been a plant from the Ninjutsu mission. Under the scrutiny of questioning and the threat of jail time, the operative had fessed up. His role had been to attach a communication device to the drone, activate it in his hotel room, and then leave on the same day. A multitude of electronics equipment had been found in his hotel room when Icelandic police escorted him there for a search.

The idea was simple, and the technology to pull it off was sophisticated. Once the communication device was attached to the drone, it would link by wireless signal between the drone and the base computer hub. Data would be captured and sent remotely to the Ninjutsu mission's master computer in Shanghai. The communication device would then act as a spy satellite by gathering player information. This vital intelligence would provide competing countries with data profiling on key players likely to be used in international tournaments. The Chinese Football Federation could access player strengths, weaknesses, tactics, and positioning to build tactical team responses during matches.

It was a high-risk situation for the Icelandic Football Federation, considering the investment they had made in the PVI system over the years. It was all about the need for countries to dominate the world's most popular sport for political reasons, whether at home or on the international stage.

Robby needed to report his concerns to his sporting body in Australia and ensure security was at the right level. After careful consideration, he didn't entertain the offer for

Harry to play in the Chinese Super League, and he let it fall by the wayside.

He had arranged to meet Gunnar in the pressroom of Shanghai Stadium before the semi-final kickoff. It was the match between Australia and the United States. Later that day, just before kickoff, Gunnar came barging into the pressroom, huffing and puffing until he found Robby.

"I have some concerning news," Gunnar said.

"You look very worried. What's happened?"

"It's the drone. It's gone, disappeared off our system during an assessment in Keflavík just hours ago."

"What do you mean, disappeared?" He gently grabbed Gunnar's arm so he could calm him down. He wasn't making sense.

"Well, that's the issue, and we don't know where it is. Gone . . . just like that," Gunnar said. He was restless and stuttering.

"Do you suspect foul play?"

"You mean the Ninjutsu operatives?" Gunnar paused for a moment. "I'm not ruling anything out at this point."

"Are the authorities looking for it in Iceland?"

"We have people on the ground searching as we speak. It's strategically sensitive for Icelandic football. It's a big deal, and I had to take a call from the sports minister." Gunnar said.

Robby tried again to calm him down. "It could be nothing. It could have crashed into the countryside." He was trying to be rational and could sense the worry in Gunnar's tone.

"The drone has an emergency beacon if it crashes."

"And?"

"The emergency beacon didn't activate. So, at this point, I am ruling out a crash."

"So what's your gut feeling?"

"I think the drone has been hijacked."

"I'm sure that's the worst scenario. Maybe we need to wait and not jump to conclusions." Robby was trying hard to reassure him.

"I am concerned it could end up in the wrong hands. It's my greatest fear."

"Of course, I share your concerns." He looked directly at Gunnar and leaned forwards. "Let's stay calm and wait. Maybe someone will find it and let us know soon."

"I don't know . . . " Gunnar wasn't convinced.

"Look, the match is about to start. Let's take our seats." He pointed to the area reserved for press and technical staff.

Gunnar agreed, and they walked together to their seats. His mobile phone was his only real-time connection with Iceland, and he checked it feverishly for updates on the missing drone. The players were walking onto the pitch and lining up for their national anthems. The stadium was 80 percent full, and the atmosphere was building.

"Getting another call from Iceland. Excuse me for one moment," Gunnar said. He was anticipating the worst, and his hand trembled while grasping the phone.

The call lasted around two minutes before he returned to his seat. His hand was shaking as he dropped the phone between the seats trying desperately to retrieve it.

"So, what's the status? Any further updates?"

Gunnar half grinned. "Whoever hijacked the drone used it for a communications dump. They tried to steal all the player algorithms in the system by linking to the drone. They tried to make a connection and break-in."

"Sounds like it was sophisticated and well planned."

"Well, they didn't get too far with it." Gunnar's half-grin turned into a smile. "I have contingencies in the hub system that prevents unauthorised activity, and it worked. I blocked them."

Robby smiled back at Gunnar. He was pleased for him. "Your contingency plan kicked into place, and you foiled their attempts to infiltrate the system."

"Well, we still can't locate the drone and the emergency beacon." Gunnar paused momentarily. "It's possible they may have stolen it, and we will never find it again." He sat back in his seat and repeatedly caressed his beard. "Iceland is a remote and desolate country. It will be hard to find them if they are still there."

"Was it the Mark II drone or the older version?"

"Fortunately, it was the older version without the updated patch. Even though there is enough proprietary technology in this drone to make it is useful for someone to replicate."

"Your concerned they could disassemble it?"

"Yes, it would not be hard to."

"Let's hope you find it soon." He was concerned for Gunnar because he understood the significance of losing years of research to a malicious group.

"If it gets into the wrong hands and they work out the technology underpinning it, we could see a tilting in the balance of world football domination in a couple of years," Gunnar said.

Robby agreed the impact of this loss would become evident at the next World Cup tournament in two years. It was more than enough time for another nation to significantly improve its team and change the balance of power on the world football stage.

Was it the Chinese operatives associated with Mission: Ninjutsu or some other group that had hijacked the drone? Robby believed it was a well-conceived, coercive act. Only time would tell who had stolen the drone and why. The dynamics of world football power could well be on the verge of a political shift. The World Cup of 2052 would become the litmus test for international football domination. That journey leading up to 2052 had just begun for Gunnar and Robby, and they were in for a tumultuous ride.

The End

About the Author

Anthony Ranieri is a Melbourne-based professional with a bachelor's degree in human resources, and he has extensive experience working in senior corporate positions in that capacity. He has written many business articles on the topic of job hunting. Tandem Press in Australia and New Zealand published his first book, *How to Find a Job in 6 Weeks*, in 2003.

Anthony is a football aficionado and, during his spare time, was an active referee for over ten years before retiring from the profession. He has coached football at the junior level and followed the careers of his children in the sport as a parent. The idea of writing a book about his passion for football bloomed a long time ago, and this is his first work in the football genre. He welcomes any questions or comments about the book at his email address, anthonyranieri@bigpond.com.

You can stay updated on the progress of volume two of *World Football Domination—The Virtual Talent Scout* at his Amazon author page: amazon.com/author/anthonyranieri.

52516952R00085

Made in the USA
Lexington, KY
15 September 2019